A Cure for Cancer

Michael Moorcock was born in London in 1939. He
contributed to and edited numerous juvenile
magazines before becoming editor of the influential
science fiction magazine *New Worlds* in 1964, a
position which he relinquished in 1971. His novels
(some fifty books carry his name) have earned him a
considerable international reputation; among the most
notable of these are *Behold the Man* (which won a
Nebula award in 1967); the fantasy novels in the Elric,
Dancers at the End of Time, Hawkmoon and Corum
series; the much-praised Jerry Cornelius tetralogy
(*The Final Programme*, *A Cure for Cancer*, *The English
Assassin* and the winner of the 1977 *Guardian* Fiction
Prize, *The Condition of Muzak*); and the romance
Gloriana, or the Unfulfill'd Queen.

A Cure
for Cancer

A Jerry Cornelius novel

Michael Moorcock

Illustrated by Malcolm Dean

Fontana/Collins

First published in Great Britain by
Allison and Busby Ltd 1971
This revised edition first published by
Fontana Paperbacks 1979

Copyright © Michael Moorcock 1971

Made and printed in Great Britain by
William Collins Sons & Co. Ltd, Glasgow

THE JERRY CORNELIUS TETRALOGY

The Final Programme (1965)
A Cure for Cancer (1968)
The English Assassin (1972)
The Condition of Muzak (1976)

Although these books may be read in any order, the reader might wish to know that the structure of this the last volume reflects the structure of the overall tetralogy. The following books are directly related to the above:

The Chinese Agent (1970)
The Nature of the Catastrophe (1971)
The Lives and Times of Jerry Cornelius (1966-74)
The Adventures of Una Persson and Catherine Cornelius in the Twentieth Century (1976)

Most other books are indirectly related, particularly:

The Warlord of the Air (1971)
The Land Leviathan (1975)
The Dancers at the End of Time (3 vols 1972-6)
Legends from the End of Time (2 vols 1976-7)
Breakfast in the Ruins (1971)

For Langdon Jones

Acknowledgments

Parts of this novel originally appeared in *Fate, Prediction, Record Mirror, New Worlds, Billboard, Headquarters Detective, True Life Confessions, The Village Voice, Guns and Ammo, Scientific American, Time, Interavia, Motorcycle Mechanics, TV and Movie Play, Man's Magazine, Screen and TV Album, New Man, Silver Screen, Titbits, The Observer, Reveille, The Plain Truth, Science Horizons, Daily Sketch, Vogue* and other British and American magazines and newspapers to whom acknowledgments are gratefully made.

Note to the reader

This book has been revised for the present Fontana edition. It has an unconventional structure and, like the other books in the tetralogy (like the overall tetralogy itself), is developed and resolved in something approximating sonata form: Introduction; Development (1 and 2); Resolution; Coda.

Contents

1. DIAGNOSIS

'Terror is the most effective political instrument ... I shall spread terror by the surprise employment of all my measures. The important thing is the sudden shock of an overwhelming fear of death.'

Adolf Hitler

Preliminary Consultation

'HERE on the top of a modern and reputable London store lives a garden of incredible beauty one hundred feet above Kensington High Street – the shopping centre of the Royal Borough of Kensington – The gardens embrace some 1½ acres, and comprise an Old English Garden, Tudor Courts and flower beds, and a Spanish Garden with Moorish pergolas and a Court of Fountains.'

DERRY & TOMS FAMOUS ROOF GARDEN

1. A Troll Across the Rooftops

The time might be July 31st 1970.

London, England. Cool traffic circulates. A quiet, hot day: somewhere in the distance – a bass tone.

In High Street, Kensington, where the trees of Hyde Park creep out among the buildings, stands the age-old structure of the Derry and Toms department store. Tier upon impressive tier, it is proud among its peers.

On the roof of the store, in a lot of rich earth, grow shrubs and trees and flowers, and there are little streams and ponds with goldfish and ducks. Who better to describe this roofgarden than those who built it? In the 1966 edition of their brochure, Derry and Toms said:

'They are the only gardens in the world of such large dimensions at so great a height, over 100 ft. above ground level, overlooking London with St Paul's in the distance. The gardens are $1\frac{1}{2}$ acres in extent and comprise an Old English Garden, Tudor Courts and Flower Beds and a Spanish Garden with Moorish Pergolas and A Court of Fountains. The water for the fountains, the river and the waterfall, is drawn from our Artesian Wells 400 ft. deep. The depth of the soil averages 2 ft. 6 in. and the distribution of weight of this and the masonry used was arranged by the Company's architect when planning the Derry and Toms building. The Gardens took three years to build and were opened in May 1938 by the Earl of Athlone, KG.

'From the balconies that adjoin the gardens you have the opportunity of enjoying the most magnificent views of London. You can see the spires and towers of the Kensington Museums, the great Dome of St. Pauls, Westminster Abbey and Westminster Cathedral – the Albert Hall, Albert Memorial, etc.'

In order, the captions to the pictures read:
  1. A delightful view of the Court of Fountains
  2. The water for the fountains, the river and the waterfall is

drawn from our artesian wells four hundred feet deep. The
depth of soil averages 2 feet 6 inches and the distribution
of weight of this and the masonry was arranged by the
company's architect when planning the Derry and Toms
building.

3. The Spanish Gardens
4. Fully matured fruit-bearing trees stretch up towards the
   sky.
5. Aerial view of the Spanish Garden where palm-trees and
   grape-vines live the year round.
6. Corner of the Spanish Garden showing the Well of St
   Theresa in a cobbled court – with vine-covered walls.
7. Another view of the Spanish garden – showing the spire of
   St Mary Abbots Church in the background.
8. (*Opposite*) The magnificent Court of Fountains
9. Flowers bloom in profusion and green lawns flourish.
10. (*Below*) The Tudor Gardens
11. Views of the Spanish Gardens
12. The campanile and convent with fountain in foreground –
    so typically Spanish in atmosphere.
13. Vine-covered archways leading to the Court of Fountains
    – all this one hundred feet above the traffic of London!
14. *This garden has a world of pleasure in't*

                                                (SHAKESPEARE)

15. The Tudor Gardens
16. Entrance to the Tudor Gardens – you go back through
    history to the beginning of the sixteenth century.
17. Henry VIII might well have wandered through this garden
    and plucked a red rose for Anne Boleyn.
18. Another view of the Tudor Gardens and its carved stone
    archways and red brick paving.
19. *A waterfall feeds a meandering stream.*
20. Ducks on the Woodland Garden lawn
21. The Sun Pavilion Restaurant with its umbrella-shaded
    balconies – a modern restaurant in the quiet setting of an
    English garden.
22. The waterfall – shaded by quiet trees alive with the gur-
    gling of water and the twittering of the birds – like a ren-
    dezvous in the country.
23. Again the Sun Pavilion Restaurant – here you will find

peace and pleasure – high above London – overlooking the Woodland Gardens.

On summer afternoons ill-clad ladies wander through the gardens; they wear felt and fluffy nylon hats, suits of linen or rayon or double jersey, bright scarves tied cowboy fashion about their throats. The place is the last retreat in London of the female of an old and dying English race – the 'Waites-dwellers' as they have often been called, although many live in pre-Waites communities and some do not always own Austins. She comes to Derry's when her shopping is done in Barkers or Pontings (they are all next to each other in the High Street); only here may she with some certain safety take her middle-class tea.

There are walls about the retreat. One wall has a locked gate. The key to the gate is owned by the man who secretly owns the chain of stores on this block, as well as other similiar substantial properties throughout London.

Now, below, we hear the sound of drowsy mid-afternoon traffic. The banner of D&T hangs limp against its staff. Not far away is the Kensington Gardens Hotel and the Kensington Strip, with its bazaars and eateries and bright lights. Not far from the Strip, to the west, is secluded Kensington Palace Gardens, vulgarly called Millionaire's Row, the avenue of the Embassies, running beside Kensington Gardens where the statue of Peter Pan still plays its pipes near the sparkling Serpentine. Derry and Toms faces towards North Kensington, the largest and most densely populated part of the Royal Borough, the most delicious slum in Europe.

It is almost tea-time.

2. 'Broken Blossoms' Lover in Garden Sex Fest ! ! !

Within the vine-covered walls of the Dutch garden the sultry sun beat down on colourful flowers and shrubs.

There were tulips like blue velvet, tulips of red, yellow, white and mauve; daffodils; pink and scarlet roses, chrysanthemums, rhododendrons, peonies. All the flowers were bright and all the scents were sweet.

The air was hot and still; there was not a trace of a breeze; but in one part of the garden a patch of cream daffodils began to move; they soon became violently agitated, as if invisible stallions galloped through them. Stems bent and broke. Then the daffodils stopped moving.

Almost immediately a nearby field of white and red tulips began to shake and thresh.

There was the smell of lilac, very heavy on the air, and the tulips groaned, leaves slapping against leaves.

When they had stopped, the roses in the next bed fluttered and bent, scarlet petals falling fast, thorns tearing, branches shuddering.

Finally, when the roses were calm again, a huge bed of mixed snap-dragons, pansies, meadowsweet, ivy-leaved toad-flax, irises, hollyhocks, narcissi, violets and sunflowers burst into life; petals shot into the sky, leaves erupted in all directions; there was a great, wild, lush, ululating noise; then silence.

Lying between damp, ivory thighs, Jerry Cornelius sighed and smiled into the unseeing face of Captain Hargreaves, member of the US military advisory commission in Europe and a fine greedy girl.

Jerry's skin, as black as a Biafran's, glistened, and he thought about all the kinds of girls he had known as he took in the flowers above his head and then Flora Hargreaves's slowly cooling eyes. He rolled like the surf; reached across the soft earth for a cigarette.

A bass tone. He glanced at the sky. It was clear.

When he looked back Flora's eyes had closed and she was sleeping, her auburn hair burnishing the pillow of crushed petals, her perfect face at perfect peace, the sweat drying on her sweet body. He bent and lightly kissed her left breast, touched her smooth shoulder, got up and went to find her uniform where she had folded it beside the patch of cream daffodils.

A man in his late twenties, with a healthy, muscular body, a large Liberty's neo-Art Nouveau wrist-watch as a bangle on either wrist; his skin was ebony and his hair not blond but milk white. Jerry Cornelius was a revolutionary of the old school.

Humming an early Jimi Hendrix number (*Foxy Lady*), Jerry sought his own clothes. He found them on the grass close to Flora's olive duds. On top of the pile lay his chromium-plated vibragun which he now picked up and holstered, strapping the holster to his naked body. He pulled on his lavender shirt, his red underpants, his red socks, his midnight-blue Cardin trousers with the flared bottoms, the matching double-creased high-waisted jacket; he smoothed his long white hair, took a mirror from his pocket and adjusted his wide purple tie, looking at his face as an afterthought.

A very *negative* appearance, he thought, pursing his lips and smiling. He picked up Flora's uniform and laid it near her; then he walked through the sunlight and flowers, knee-deep, towards the garden gate.

3. Wild Whirlybird in One Man War!!

Beyond the wall the middle-class woman walked the pleasant paths, glancing nervously or with disapproval at the creature who, as if he owned the place, locked the gate behind him. They mistook him for a dandified Negro, and thought it likely that he was responsible for the increasingly loud bass tone: he carried something rather like a transistor radio.

Jerry put the key in his pocket and wandered in the direction of the Woodland Garden which, with its streams and shady trees, was flanked by the Sun Pavilion Restaurant which was not yet open.

He passed several black doors marked *Emergency Exit* and paused by the lift, murmuring a word to the attendant and the ticket girl. They nodded. The girl entered the lift and with an air of finality it descended.

Jerry turned back to the Woodland Garden. As he reached it the bass tone sounded very close and he looked up and saw the helicopter, moving in low, up over the outer wall, its rotors thrashing, the leaves of the trees whipping off their branches, the petals of the flowers flung about in all directions.

The women screamed, wondering what to do.

Jerry drew his vibragun. He knew an enemy helicopter when he saw one.

The chopper was huge, over forty feet long, and flying close to the tops of the trees, its deep-throated motor full of menace, its shadow over the gardens.

Jerry moved swiftly across the open space towards the tree-shaded lawn of the Woodland Glade, the leaves stinging his face.

A machine gun hissed and slim bullets bit the concrete. Jerry rested his vibragun across his bent right arm and took aim, but he could hardly see his great target for the whistling petals and leaves that lashed his face. He stumbled backwards into a pool, slipped and found himself waist-deep in cold water. There were almost no leaves on the trees now as the rotors flicked

20

round and round.

Someone began to shout through a megaphone at him. 'Fuckpig! Fuckpig! Fuckpig!'

The old ladies gasped and ran about in panic, finding the lift out of order and the emergency exits blocked. They huddled under the arches of the Tudor Garden or threw themselves flat behind the low walls of the Spanish Garden.

Some of the copter's bullets hit a group of noisy ducks and blood and feathers mingled with the flying leaves. Rather half-heartedly, Jerry fired back.

The chopper – a Westland Whirlwind with the 750 hp Alvis Leonides Major engine – banked slightly until it was hovering over a clear space in which a fountain splashed. It began to drop lower, its 53 ft rotors barely missing the trees.

The machine gun hissed again and Jerry was forced to fling himself under the water and slide along until he could crouch beneath a small stone bridge. A man jumped from the copter, cradling the gun in his arms. He began to trudge towards the point where Jerry had gone down. There was blood on the surface, but it was the blood of ducks and doves.

Jerry smiled. He aimed his vibragun at the man with the machine gun. The man began to tremble. The machine gun fell apart in his hands; he shook violently and collapsed.

The copter was beginning to rise. Jerry dashed for it. 'Easy,' he called. 'Easy.'

There could be as many as nine people in the copter, apart from the pilot. He dived through the hatch. Save for the fallen megaphone, it was empty. Above him, the pilot stared at him through goggles. The copter gained height.

Jerry put his head out of the hatch. Frightened ladies, their hats like so many coloured dollops of cream, wailed up at him. 'We're stranded! We can't get out! We'll starve! Hooligan! Go back to your own country! Help!'

'Don't worry,' Jerry called as the copter climbed. He picked up the megaphone. 'The restaurant opens soon. Please form an orderly queue. It will assist everyone if you try to behave in a normal manner! In the meantime ...' He flung his taper to the soft ground. It began to play a selection of George Formby's greatest hits, including *When I'm Cleaning Windows*, *Fanlight Fanny* and *Auntie Maggie's Remedy*. 'And don't for-

get Old Mother Riley, Max Miller and Max Wall! It is for them that you suffer today!'

As the helicopter thrummed out of sight, the ladies murmured among themselves and their lips curled in disgust as George Formby sang about the tip of his little cigar, but they formed a long, disciplined queue outside the restaurant.

Eight days later they would still be standing there, or sitting, or lying where they had fallen. Through the glass walls of the restaurant they had been able, every day between three o'clock and five o'clock, to see the waitresses laying out the little sandwiches, scones and cakes and later clearing them away again. If a lady signalled a waitress the waitress would wave, smile apologetically and point at the notice which said that the restaurant was closed.

One plump middle-aged housewife in a blue paisley suit hugged her handbag to her stomach in disapproval. The George Formby songs, rather scratchy now, were still going. 'I feel filthy,' she said. 'It's wicked ...'

'Don't start a fuss, dear.'

On the lawn, quacking cheerfully, forgetful of their earlier upsets, jolly ducks waddled about.

4. Sing to Me, Darling, in Our Castle of Agony

'Drop me off at Earls Court, would you?' Jerry asked, stroking the pilot's neck with his vibragun.

Pettishly the chopper sank towards the flat roof of the Beer-A-Gogo, recently built on the site of the old Billabong Club, and hovered there with undisguised impatience.

Jerry opened the hatch and jumped out, falling elegantly through the thin asbestos sheeting and landing with a bump on mouldy sacks of flour that filled his nostrils with a sour smell. Rats scattered and turned to watch him from the shadows. He sighed and got up, dusting his suit, watching, through the jagged hole, the helicopter disappearing into the sky.

Jerry left the storeroom and stood on the landing listening to the lusty sounds from below. The migrants were celebrating 'Piss on a Pom' week, getting drunk on home brewed beer or 'pickling Percy's plums' as they put it.

Jerry could hear them laughing a great deal as the jokes flew back and forth: 'That's a beaut drop of *beer*, mate!'

'I'm telling you, drong, that sheila was like a flaming glass of cold *beer*!'/'Watch you don't spill your fucking *beer* sport!'

Some of the lusty singing was also about beer or its absence. The migrants seemed fully absorbed. Jerry walked softly downstairs and sneaked past the main room. He was momentarily dazzled by the electric blue drape suits (Kings Cross Blues) but managed to make the front door into Warwick Avenue, full of Dormobiles, Volkswagen mini-buses and Land-Rovers covered in pictures of kangaroos, emus and kiwis, all marked FOR SALE.

Jerry tossed a silver yen to a Negro boy with a face daubed in white clay. 'Can you find a cab?'

The boy swaggered around a corner and came back at a run. He was followed by a skinny horse drawing a Lavender Cab, its bright paint peeling to reveal old brown varnish and its upholstery cracked and bursting. The gaunt young man on the box wore a long beard and a fur hat; he signalled with his whip for Jerry to climb into the hansom which rocked and creaked as Jerry got aboard.

Then the whip cracked over the jutting bones of the horse; it lurched forward, snorted and began to gallop down the street at enormous speed. Jerry clung on as the cab rocked from side to side and hurtled across an intersection. From over his head he heard a strange, wild droning and realized that the driver was singing in time to the rhythm of the horse's hooves. The tune seemed to be *Auld Lang Syne* and only after a while did Jerry realize that the song was a favourite of the 1917–21 war.

'We're here because we're here because we're here,' sang the driver, 'because we're here. We're here because we're here because we're here because we're here. We're here because we're here because we're here because we're here. We're here because we're here because we're here because we're here. We're here because we're here because we're here because we're here. We're here because we're here because we're here because we're here. We're here because we're here because we're here because we're here. We're here because we're here because we're here. We're here because we're here because we're here because we're here. We're here because we're here because we're here.'

Jerry pushed up the trapdoor in the roof and shouted at the

singing, glassy-eyed face, giving his address. The driver continued to drone, but gave a sharp tug on the reins and the cab turned, flinging Jerry to his seat and making the trap shut with a thud.

'We're here because we're here because we're here because we're here. We're here because we're here. We're here because we're here because we're here because we're here.' Through the west London streets, all desolate and beautiful in the soft tree-filtered sunlight, to the high walled fortress in Ladbroke Grove that had once housed the Convent of the Poor Clares, a closed order. Jerry had bought it from the Catholic Church shortly before the reformation. Behind the heavy metal gates topped by electrified barbed wire came the sound of the Beatles singing *Back in the U.S.S.R.* Jerry got out of the cab and before he could pay, the driver had whipped up the horse and was off towards Kilburn, his high voice still singing.

'*Dear Prudence, won't you come out to play.*' Jerry rested his palm on the recognition plate and the gate opened. He glanced, as usual, at the slogan 'Vietgrove' painted on the north wall of the convent. It had been there for two years and continued to puzzle him. It didn't seem to be the work of the regular slogan painters.

Crossing the elm-lined courtyard to the bleak, brick house, Jerry heard a tortured scream coming from one of the barred upper windows and recognized the voice of his latest charge (whom he had come to take to the country), an ex-chairman of the Arts Council of Great Britain, well-known in the early forties as a heavy playing opposite Humphrey Bogart, and now awaiting a crash transmog.

A tricky customer, thought Jerry.

5. Mystery of Yowling Passenger in Snob Auto

Jerry drove the Phantom VI convertible at a rapid lick. The controls of the car, beautifully designed in diamonds, rubies and sapphires by Gilian Packard, responded with delicate sensuality to his touch. In the back, in his chamois leather straitjacket, the transmog case continued to scream.

'EEEEEEEEEEEEEEEEEEEEEEEEEEEEEEEEEEEEEEEEEHELP MEEEEEEEEEEEEEEEEEEEEEEEEEEEEEEEEEEEEEEEEEEEE.'

'That's what we're trying to do, old lord. Hang on.'

'Aaaaaaaaaaaaahh! Why? Why? Aaaaaaaaaaaaaaaaaaaaaaaaaaa aaaaaaaaaaaaaaaa why aaaaaaaaaaaaaaaaaaaaaaaaaaaaaaaaaaaaaa aaaaaaaaaaaaaaaaaaaaaaaaaaaaawhyaaaaaaaaaaaaaaaaaaawhyaaaaaa whyaaaaaaaaaaaaaaaaaaaaaaaaaaaaaaaaaaaaaaawhyaaaaaaaa ahhhh! YOU WON'T GET AWAY WITH THIS, YOUNG MAN! Yaaaaaaaaaaaaaaaaaaaaaaaaaaaaaaaaaaaaaaaaaaaaa! You'll regret thisaaaaaaaaaaaaaaaaaaaaaaaaaaaaaaaaaa! WHY! WHY! WHY! AAAAAAAAAAAAAH! Yaaaaaaaaaaaaaaaaaaaaaaaaaaaaargh! Yaaaaaaaaaaaaaaaaaaaaaaaaaaaaaaaaaaaaaaaaaaaaaaaaaaaargh! THE AUTHORITIES WILL SOON CATCH UP WITH *YOU*, MY FRIEND! OOOOOOOOOOOOOOOOOOOOOOOO OOOOOOOOOOOOOOH. URSH! YAROOOOOOOOOOOOO! I SAY, STOP IT, YOU ROTTERS! OOOOOOOOOOOOCH! GAARR! EEEEEEEEEEEEEEEEEEEEEEEEEEEEEEEEEEEEEEE EEEEEEEEEEEEEEEEEEEK! *DO YOU KNOW WHO I AM??????*'

'Do you? That's what we're trying to fix. Be quiet, there's a good chap.'

'AAAAAAAAAAAAAAAAAAAAAAAAAAAAAAAAAAAAAAAA
AAAAAAAAAAAAAAAAAAAAAAAAAAAAAAAAAAAAAAAA
AAAAAAAAAAAAAAAAAAAAAAAAAAAAAAAAAAAAAAAA

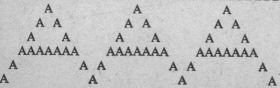

AAAAAAAAAAAAAAAAAAAAAAAAAAAAAAAAAAAAAAAAAAA
AAAAAAAAAAAAAAAAAAAAAAAAAAAAAAAAAAAAAAAAAAA
AAAAAAAAAAAAAAAAAAAAAAAAAAAAAAAAAAAAAAAAAAA
HHHHHHHHH!' said the ex-chairman defiantly.

Jerry pursed his lips and touched the ruby stud of his taper, adjusted sapphire and diamond controls for balance, and turned up the volume. Soon the passenger's voice was more or less drowned by *Everybody's Got Something to Hide Except Me and My Monkey.*

Jerry winked at his black face in the overhead mirror.

6. Dangerous Dude's Dream of Destruction

'Don't worry, we'll soon have him in the fuzz box,' smiled the kindly old matron as Jerry said goodbye to her at the main door of the Sunnydale Reclamation Centre. The matron had formerly been a Greek millionairess, famous for her escapades, and had known the new client in the old days when he had holidayed aboard her yacht *Teddy Bear*. She handed Jerry the latest issue of *The Organ* (*A Quarterly Review for its Makers, its Players & its Lovers*). 'This came for you today – at the house.'

'No other mail?'

'Not to my knowledge.'

Jerry put the magazine in his pocket and waved goodbye. In the peaceful grounds of the Centre the day was warm and beautiful. His silky pink Phantom VI stood in the drive, contrasting nicely with the grey and yellow gravel. Pines and birches lined the drive and behind them Jerry could see the red roof of his little Dutch mansion which he'd had shipped from Holland in the days before the blockade.

He leapt into the Phantom VI and was away, touching seventy as he passed the gates and hurtled into the road in the path of a slow silver Cadillac that pulled up sharply as he turned and zoomed off towards the metropolis, his milk-white hair streaming in the wind.

The sweet music of a thousand hidden radio transmitters filled the countryside and brought heavenly sound to the pastoral landscape. Such harmony, thought Jerry contentedly, that only the Beatles could achieve; such a perfect combination. From the circle of US and Russian Navy radio ships surrounding and protecting Britain, the same synchronized record played to all the people everywhere. Was there ever such a Utopia? he wondered as he left the subsidiary road and hit the main drag, joining the racing rainbow stream of cars on the multilane highway.

Overhead, like birds of paradise, swarmed the flying

machines, the little helicopters, gliders, rocket chairs, pedi-planes, air taxis, light aircraft of every variety, belonging to the comfortably-off (and who was not in these delightful Home Counties?), flowing towards London where gleaming towers of all colours could be seen in the distance.

Was it fair, Cornelius asked himself, relaxing for a moment, to scheme the destruction of so much of this life, happiness and colour? It was a shame that his mission in life conflicted with it; but he was a man of will and integrity, not without a marked moral sensibility, and his first loyalty was to his organization. He was a total convert and he couldn't afford to relax until there were a few more around.

And his adventures were really only about to begin.

Tissue Sample

Clean air and economical electricity are two good reasons to celebrate Nuclear Week. Here are four more.
Clean air from clean energy.
Economical energy, too.
Nuclear-powered egg-poacher.
Suddenly it's 1980.
Nuclear crime detection – a fifth reason.
Nuclear Week for your kids – three more ways to celebrate.

Headings, Con Edison ad

1. 50,000 Victims of Kill-Crazy
   Prince Charming

Beale, claws together under his chin, eyed Jerry Cornelius only for a moment then moved suddenly, rising and falling across the room on his flamingo legs, the woollen frock coat, which was Burton's latest autumn offer, rumpling and floating. 'I am really an antiquarian.'

The room was long, lined with bound newspapers, the ceiling so large and heavy that it seemed about to fall with a thud. Cornelius glanced upwards and settled warily into the swivel armchair, knowing that, if the ceiling did fall, even he would not have a chance of surviving.

'Which volume? We have fifty thousand.' Beale's sibilant voice took a long time to reach Jerry. 'Records of the past.'

'The names,' murmured Jerry, ready to slip hand to vibragun if the situation demanded.

'London, the city of dolorous mist,' hissed Beale. 'The names, Mr Cornelius, yes; the confidential names. You say he's called S?'

'According to the Cheka.'

'Nothing else?'

'Something in code about a mouse strangler of Munich, I'm told. But that could be a reference to an anagram of Mephistophilis ...'

'Catching, Mr Aserinsky, hmph,' Beale spoke as if in reply to a question, and began to cough.

'Not in my book, general. It's oh, oh, five and wild skidoo.'

'Unused – unusual ...' Beale was puzzled, as well he might be.

It was only a ruse on Jerry's part to get into the library, but he could not move yet, could not be certain that the ceiling would not fall; and he suspected the chair.

He got up. Beale gasped, hastily reaching for a file.

Jerry knew it was now or never.

He drew the chromium-plated vibragun from its silken holster and pointed it at Beale who fell on his knees and began to shake.

When Beale had shaken to pieces, Jerry slid the warm gun back in place, stepped over the corpse, checked doors and the many windows, and got to work, pulling the bound volumes from their shelves until every last one was on the floor. Wading through this rubble, he picked one up and opened it. As he expected it contained six months' issues of the *Sunday Times Colour Supplement*. It would do to start with.

From his pocket he extracted matches and a tin of lighter fluid, squirted the fluid over the book and lit it. The rest of the fluid he squirted at random over the piles of newspapers. A little blow at History.

Someone was coming.

He ran to the door and drew the bolts; ran, stumbling, to the doors at the far end of the gallery and bolted those too. The fire was beginning to take hold. It was getting warm. He drew his vibragun and gave the huge central window a touch of ultrasonics so that it shattered instantly and he was through it, peering down into the misty street.

Swinging himself onto the ledge, he began to slide down the drainpipe, scraping the heel of his right hand quite nastily, and reached the ground where his Phantom VI, its motor turning over, waited for him.

Two or three streets away, he stopped for a moment and looked back and upwards to where he could see the white stone of the library building and the orange flames and rich, black smoke that whipped and boiled from the window he had broken. Farewell to precedent.

Sabotage was only a sideline with Jerry Cornelius, but he prided himself that he was good at it.

'What do you achieve,' a girl had once asked him, stroking the muscles of his stomach, 'what do you achieve by the destruction of the odd library? There are so many. How much can one man do?'

'What he can,' Cornelius had told her, rolling on her. 'It's History that's caused all the trouble in the past.'

Jerry glanced at the huge green-dialled watch on his left wrist. 14.41.

He sent the Phantom VI racing forward, heading away from

the City, his headlamps changing the colour of the mist rather than piercing it. Muscles and silk rippled together as he raised one jet-black hand to smooth his white hair from the jet-black forehead. He swung the wheel suddenly to avoid the back of a bus, hooted his horn as he passed on into the mist, finger-tips on wheel. Tower Bridge was ahead, open to traffic, and he raced over it, made the Elephant and Castle roundabout, whisked round it and reached eighty miles an hour as he passed over Waterloo Bridge where the mist was thinner, and the West End, whose great, jewelled towers were the city's distinctive feature, was ahead of him.

'Oh, *psychedelic*!' he murmured.

He had to be in Greek Street in five minutes. He would make it easily now.

He had to meet Spiro Koutrouboussis, his chief contact with the organization.

Koutrouboussis, one of a number of handsome young Greek millionaires who belonged to the organization, was dark-haired and slender, from Petrai originally, but now a refugee, a nationalized Israeli subject, proving just how far-sighted he was.

Leaving the thrumming Rolls in the street outside the Mercury Club, Koutrouboussis's favourite meeting place, Jerry stepped over the mist-silvered pavement and entered the warm, neon-lit club where he was greeted with some enthusiasm by the doorman who gratefully received the twenty dollar tip.

Cornelius ignored the dining part of the club, where people sat in red plush seats and ate off golden plates the finest French cuisine available anywhere in the world.

He took the stairs two at a time and bumped into Koutrouboussis who was waiting there. Koutrouboussis rubbed his side, his eyes looking rapidly from Jerry's right foot to his left and back again.

'The same old shoes, I see,' he said spitefully, and wheeled about to lead Cornelius into the private room he had on permanent hire.

2. Ex-Bank Clerk Slave Girl in Private Sin Palace

'How did you manage to get through this,' Koutrouboussis asked, burying himself in the shadows of a leather armchair by the fire while a sequined girl poured them Pernod from a gleaming decanter on her hip, 'time?'

Jerry stroked his glass. 'They thought I was a visiting disc jockey from France. It worked well enough and long enough.' There were few long-range airships and, to its joy, the nation was blockaded by the radio ships. Jerry downed the yellow drink and held out his glass. The girl was an organization convert and very successful and very happy; she smiled sweetly at Cornelius as she filled his glass; she had once been a clerk in a bank, had worn a green overall and counted money. Her place had been taken by another convert who had originally worked as a hostess just round the corner. The organization was very neat, on the whole.

Koutrouboussis's eyes glowed from the shadows as he darted a look of jealousy at Cornelius. The poor man had sacrificed himself for others, but he could not help resenting them from time to time.

'Ah,' he said.

'The organization got the French delivery?' Cornelius said. 'Thirty-two. Fifteen men, seventeen women?'

'Oh, yes. In good time,' Koutrouboussis said with a secret in his mellowing eyes.

'That was important,' Cornelius murmured. 'I'm glad. You were to settle here.'

'It's been arranged. Sixty-four thousand pounds in hard yen in your London account under the name of Aserinsky. Well worth it.'

Jerry worked on a strict commission basis. It preserved autonomy and had been part of the original contract when he had surrendered admin control to the Greeks. 'Have they been processed yet?'

'A few. It should be a successful batch, I think.'

Jerry held out his glass for another drink; Pernod was the only alcohol he really liked and in this he was a child.

'But we're having trouble,' Koutrouboussis added. 'Opposition...'

'That's not –'

'– unusual, I know. But in this case the opposition seems to realize what we're up to. I mean, they understand what we're doing.'

'A tip-off?'

'Could be. But does – it doesn't matter.'

'No.'

'This group,' continued Koutrouboussis, 'is an international one with its headquarters in America ...'

'Where else? Official?'

'I don't know. Perhaps. The difficulties ...'

'Difficult for them to operate and for us to reach them, of course. But do you ... ?'

'We don't want you to go there.'

Jerry leant back in his chair. He looked nervously at the flickering fire in the grate nearby, but it offered no danger. He relaxed.

'It's the German chapter that seems to be offering us the serious threat at this stage,' Koutrouboussis cleaned his nails with a toothpick. 'We know one of them – a woman. She's a dental surgeon living in Cologne. Already she's deconverted some half-dozen of our German people.'

'Turned them on and turned them back?'

'Exactly. The usual method. But much smoother.'

'So she's got a good idea of our process.'

'To the last detail, apparently. Some Russian source, I think – the leak. Maybe the Patriarch himself, eh?'

'You want me to kill her?'

'How you work is up to you.' Koutrouboussis fingered his lips.

Jerry's black face glistened in the firelight. He frowned. 'We'd prefer a conversion, I suppose.'

'Always. But if you can't save a soul, get rid of it.' Koutrouboussis smirked with self approval (although normally he did not at all approve of his self).

'The organization isn't in agreement on that issue,' Jerry

pointed out. 'Repent or die.'

'Quite.'

'Well. I'll see what I can do.' Jerry stroked the girl's pelvis. 'And I go to Cologne, eh?'

'It might be an idea,' Koutrouboussis said uncertainly. 'To get yourself fully in the picture – but you needn't do anything there. She's coming to Britain, we gather, shortly, to organize the British chapter.'

Unsettled by the Greek's somewhat puritanical attitude (natural, he supposed, for a man who had given up so much), Jerry drank another glass of Pernod, feeling a trifle light-headed. The flavour of the liquorice was firmly on his palate now. If he were going to enjoy his dinner, he had better stop.

'Bring me a glass of ice-water, darling, will you please?' He patted the girl's thigh.

'That would be the best time to strike,' Koutrouboussis suggested. 'Off her own territory and on yours.'

Jerry reached out for the water and drank it slowly. 'What's her name?'

'Name?'

'What's she called?'

'Name.'

Koutrouboussis made an urgent, spasmodic gesture with his right hand. He breathed heavily.

'Doctor ...' he began. 'Karen – Karen ...'

Jerry reached up and pulled the girl to him. They kissed each other firmly and pulling off their clothes lay down on the floor and fucked with hot and hasty passion.

'... von ...'

Snorting and quivering, they came.

'... Krupp.'

'What was that again?' Jerry did up his trousers.

'Dr Karen von Krupp. It's a lot to remember.'

'Got it.'

Jerry felt only pity. For some men, immortality was not enough.

'Her address in Cologne?'

'She lives outside Cologne. A small town to the west. Nibelburg. Look for the old Gothic stone tower. That's where she has her surgery.'

'So I go to her and ask her to check my teeth.' Jerry tapped his whitened choppers.

'She'll guess who you are.'

'Will she try to detail me?'

'Make sure she doesn't,' Koutrouboussis said nervously. 'Not you, Cornelius. We can't afford it.'

Jerry smiled. He could smell the first course, *moules marinière*, just before there was a knock on the door and the waiter pushed the trolley into the room.

3. US Navy Ships Turned 'Pirate'! ! !

Koutrouboussis had given him his route plan, but how he crossed from Dover to Ostend was his own affair. It was more than twenty miles of sea, and three miles out was the tight circle of well-armed US 'pirate' radio ships.

Jerry's Phantom VI, a streak of pink power on the white, sparkling road, roared through the clear sunlight of the autumn afternoon, making for Dover.

Wearing his Panda-skin coat and a white silk turban in which was set a jewelled clasp supporting a spray of peacock feathers, Jerry stretched comfortably in his seat. He was disguised sufficiently to fool a casual observer and he hoped, too, that Karen von Krupp would not immediately recognize him for what he was.

Jerry saw the bright ruin of the silver bridge that had once spanned the sea between England and France and which had collapsed in a tangle of flashing strands shortly after it had been built. Above it a metal ornithopter wheeled.

Now he could see the sea ahead, the little blue waves glinting in the sun, and the road began to slope towards it. Jerry decelerated gradually, switching controls in the convertible until, when the road slid into the sea, the Phantom VI had become a speedboat.

Gracefully, and without slackening speed, the Rolls cut across the water and before long the outlines of the ring of ships could be seen. Jerry touched another control.

This was his first opportunity to try out the car's new feature, for which he had paid a hundred and fifty thousand marks.

There was a soft, muttering sound and the Rolls-Royce began to sink beneath the ocean. It was capable of submerging only a matter of feet and for short distances, but it would probably see him through.

His speed had decreased considerably now. He peered through the murky water, looking upwards, and soon saw the keels of the radio ships ahead. Their sonar was bound to detect him and they would begin dropping depth charges almost at once, but with luck they would detonate well below him and a vessel as small as his would be hard to pin-point with any great accuracy.

They had a fix.

He saw the first charge plunge into the water on his right and fall towards the ocean bed.

Then another fell close to it, and another on his left, another behind him.

He watched them sink.

One by one the shock waves rose, threatening to blow him to the surface under the Yankee's guns.

The car rocked. Its forward course was deflected by a further series of shock waves.

Jerry kept firm control of the wheel, letting the car move with the waves, waiting until they had died before pressing on, beneath the ships' keels and beyond them.

More depth charges struck the water and floated down.

One of the blue steel canisters brushed the side of the car and he swung violently away as, below him, it exploded, catching the rear and almost turning the Rolls end over end.

Jerry was thrown forward against the wheel. Another charge went off. The water was cloudy. He lost his bearings.

The car spiralled to a dangerous depth; he managed to switch on the interior lights and regain control as he began to somersault.

Checking the instruments, he judged he was out of range. He began to rise.

Breaking through the waves, the limousine continued its stately way across the surface. Looking back, Jerry could see the ships behind him.

A few guns blew black smoke from their muzzles, he heard the roar as they fired, saw the shells splash into the sea and burst on either side of him, spraying the canopy of the car with water and momentarily making him lose visibility.

He smiled. Before they got his range, he would be over the horizon.

Until the radio ships thought of putting down anti-sub nets, the car would be useful.

Dashing like a dolphin through the warm water, the Rolls-Royce was soon in sight of Ostend and a similar concrete roadway. It hit the road smoothly under Cornelius's control, reconverted and was bowling along the road to Brussels without a moment's interruption.

He bought a paper at a roadside kiosk, saw that Israel had annexed Ukraine and that another hundred thousand US military advisors had been flown into European HQ, Bonn.

And the sun was setting.

The act of running the radio-ship blockade had tired him a trifle and he planned to spend the night at an organization-approved hotel in Brussels.

Soon Brussels lay ahead, all baroque red and gold in the sunset, sweet city of nostalgia.

Blood Sample

At Mach 3 ordinary tyres start to melt.
Goodrich ad

1. Dope Pushing Preacher was Peeping Tom

Bishop Beesley placed a bar of Turkish Delight into his large, wet mouth, smiled as he chewed the soft chocolate and jelly, and unwrapped another bar. He swallowed, licked his lips with his grey tongue, and picked up his pen.

In the lounge of The Golden Orrery, one of the best hotels in Brussels, he was polishing up the newspaper article he was writing. It was called *Heroin: A Cure for Cancer?* and would appear the following Sunday. He had written for the *Christian Science Monitor* for some years. Before the dissolution of the clergy, he had done the regular *From My Pulpit* feature, and afterwards, when the *Monitor* had to change its policy to fit in with modern trends, had changed the name of his column to *From My Viewpoint*. Journalism, however, did not pay him sufficiently and was really just a useful sideline.

From where he sat, Bishop Beesley could see the main entrance of the hotel and he looked up as the glass doors swung open. Through them came a man carrying a light grip and dressed in a black and white fur coat. The man appeared to be an Indian, for his skin was black and he wore an elaborate turban and what the bishop considered a rather vulgar silk suit. The man walked to the reception desk and spoke to the clerk who handed him a key.

The bishop popped the unwrapped bar of Turkish Delight into his mouth and resumed work.

It did not take him long to complete the article, put it into an envelope, address and stamp the envelope and walk to the hotel's mail-box where he posted it.

He looked at the clock over the reception desk and saw that dessert would be being served about now. He walked across the foyer to the dining room and entered it. The dining room was half-full. Two or three family groups sat at tables along the walls, a few business men with their wives or secretaries ate at other tables, and at the far end sat the Indian who seemed to have chosen pheasant, the hotel's speciality.

Bishop Beesley hated the whole idea of meat. He hated the whole idea of vegetables, for that matter, but the orange bombes were unmatched anywhere and it was for them that he came to The Golden Orrery.

With a great deal of dignity he sat his full buttocks down on the well-stuffed chair and put his pale hands on the cloth.

There was no need to order.

Very shortly a waiter appeared with the first of the six orange bombes that the bishop would eat tonight, as he ate every night when in Brussels.

The Bishop picked up fork and spoon and bent his nose over the dessert, his eyes watering with delight.

Although absorbed in pleasure, the bishop could not help noticing the Indian when the man got up and walked past his table. He walked so lithely, there was such a sense of physical power about him, that the bishop wondered for an instant if he were all he seemed to be.

Though he had paused only a split second in his eating, it was enough to bring the bishop back to his fourth orange bombe with added relish.

Rising, at length, from the table, he decided to get an early night. He had a busy morning to look forward to.

Jerry Cornelius took off his turban and flipped it into the chair beside the bed. Una Persson looked a little surprised by the colour of his hair; her full lips parted and she moved her body on the bed.

Like a big, black boa constrictor he slid from his silks and came slowly towards her, taking her shoulders in his strong hands, pulling her so that her pink breasts pressed against his ebony chest and she drew a deep breath before his lips touched her rose-soft mouth, his tongue stroked hers and love boiled in their bodies, rising, rising, rising in volume with the glory of the very finest Gregorian chant; tempo increasing, flesh flush against flesh, mouth against mouth, hands moving, bodies fusing, teeth biting, voices shouting fit to wake the dead.

He lay beside her with the smell of her body in his nostrils trying not to breathe too heavily so that the smell would stay there as long as possible. He put an arm around her shoulders and she settled against him, her long, fine dark brown hair brushing his skin. For a while they lay still and then he took his cigarettes from beside the bed and lit one each for them.

He had not expected to meet another organization operative in The Golden Orrery: Koutrouboussis had said nothing about it. But Una had recognized him in the corridor outside his room, though he did not know her.

'What are you doing here?' he'd asked.

'Looking for you.' Una took her opportunities while she could.

Now he said it again.

'I've just delivered a consignment,' she told him. 'On my way back to England now. It was a touchy job – all kinds of trouble. Are you looking for potentials here?'

'No.'

'Oho,' Una said knowingly.

He slid the flat of his hand over her thighs and hips, up her torso and over her right breast, stroking the nipple until it was hard; he put his cigarette out in the ashtray by the bed, took hers from her fingers and put that out too. Her excellent teeth delicately nipped his tongue as they kissed.

It was a shame they hadn't put the light out. Bishop Beesley, peering through his spy-hole in the room above, frowned. He had recognized Cornelius.

2. Danger! Hitch-Hikers Who Pose as Journalists!

Leaving the hotel the next morning, Cornelius was stopped by a shout from the corner of the street. Turning, he saw a familiar figure in the gaiters and frock-coat of a clergyman. The man was waving a small attaché case and waddling just as fast as he could.

'A moment, sir! A moment of your time!' The words were panted in a tone reminiscent of sewage warbling underground.

Cornelius paused by the Phantom VI. 'Ha,' he said. 'A moment, eh?' He wondered if this were an organization contact nobody had warned him about.

The clergyman reached him, breathing heavily, leant against the car and hastily pulled a paper bag from his pocket, taking something that looked like a chocolate cream from it and cramming it into his mouth. It seemed to help him recover.

'Birmingham,' he said.

'Indeed,' Cornelius replied.

'Beesley – from Birmingham. We met there the Easter before last.'

'I never go to Birmingham if I can help it,' said Jerry fastidiously. 'I haven't been there in four years.'

'Mr Aserinsky.' Bishop Beesley spoke with prim accusation. 'Mr Aserinsky! Come now. Birmingham. The Easter before last.'

'Before last, before last.' Jerry pursed his lips. 'Before last . . .'

'Aha!' Beesley grinned and patted his forehead with one finger. 'Aha! Memory playing tricks.'

'Certainly not!'

'Can't remember where one was at any particular moment - can one? Eh? Or, might I say, *who* one was, hm? Ha, ha!'

Cornelius put himself on his guard, ready to drag his vibra gun from its holster in a split second. But Beesley was leaning forward with a knowing smile. 'Trust me, Mr Aserinsky. We have much in common, you and I.'

'Are you from the organization . . .' Cornelius said, 'at all?'

'No. Unfortunate. But I understand the aims. And I endorse them, Mr Aserinsky.'

'I'm leaving now.' Jerry put hand to handle.

'I was going to ask you a favour.'

A yellow, single-decker tram went past on the other side of the street. Cornelius watched it from the corner of his eye.

'What was that?'

'I believe you are on your way to Germany. You'll be passing through Aachen?'

'That's for me to say.' Jerry relaxed a little as the tram turned a corner.

'Could you perhaps, give me a lift? I am only a poor journalist and the rail fares are so dear, as you appreciate, I'm sure.'

'Journalist?'

'Churchman? Unfortunately that profession is a dead one these days. Progress, Mr Aserinsky, has scant sympathy for the redundant . . . I mean,' the bishop reached into his coat pocket and took out a bar of chocolate which he put into his mouth, 'I mean – one must survive. There was little else I was trained for. Consolation was my trade. I still pursue it as best I can.'

Jerry watched a thin trickle of chocolate leave Bishop Beesley's mouth. It looked rather like blood.

'I don't trust you,' he said.

'Forgive a trace of self-pity.' The bishop spread his hands and shrugged in despair. 'But my appearance is doubtless disturbing to you. Can I help that? My clothes – they are all I have. My poor, coarse body: glands. My method of approach: urgent necessity, if I am to earn the pittance that will support me for another week or two. And there is the plague to consider. Rats have been seen. You, Mr Aserinsky, *are well dressed, handsome, rich too . . .*'

'Too rich.' Jerry opened the door and threw his grip into the back of the car. He slid into the driving seat, closed the door of the car and started the engine.

Soon he was driving from Brussels, on the Aachen road.

Not too far behind him, his face set in an expression of moral outrage, came Bishop Beesley, stiff-backed at the wheel of a silver Cadillac, his jaw moving rhythmically and, from time to time, his hand moving to meet it. Beside him on the seat was a large paper bag containing almost a pound of walnut fudge.

Bishop Beesley turned to walnut fudge in moments of crisis.

Analysis

> *La liberté ne sera recouvrés,*
> *L'occupera noir, fier, vilain, inique,*
> *Quand la matière du pont sera ouvrée,*
> *D'Hister, Venise fasche la republique.* (5.29)

In his book *Prophecies on World Events by Nostradamus* (Liveright Publications Inc., 1961) Stephen Robb tells us that Hister is an old name for the Danube. But the passage of the centuries, he says, has brought it up to date. He believes that it was an obvious word for the prophet to use, for it meant the Danube and also served as an anagram of Hitler. Mr Robb says that in the sixteenth century anagrams were as popular as crossword puzzles are today. *Hister*, therefore, with one letter change gives us *Hitler*. Mr Robb says that the change of one letter was permissible in anagram writing (see *Dictionnaire de Trevoux*). What other word, asks Mr Robb, can serve better than *Hister* to specify both the name, and the place of origin of 'the bold, black, base-born, iniquitous man' who was to 'occupy liberty'?

1. Blonde Mistress of Nibelburg's
Tower of Terror!

Jerry passed through Aachen listening to Olivier Messiaen's *Turangalila Symphony* on his headphones. He frowned self-critically as the seventh movement began. His Ondes Martenot playing was dreadful. He hardly noticed the F111A nose-dive into a nearby field until the sight of the flames made him stop the car and watch as the US Marines arrived in three Shawnee whirlybirds and, automatic weapons at the ready, ringed the wreck. One of the advisors jerked his thumb at Jerry to continue down the road. He waved, wound back to the beginning of the movement and was once again on his way to Nibelburg with a couple of hours to go and by this time aware of the Cadillac on his tail. The bishop was apparently making no attempt to hide the fact that he was pursuing Jerry.

Cornelius waited until the marines were out of sight and then decided to give Bishop Beesley the slip.

At the touch of a button the Phantom VI sprouted stubby wings and tail section, the turbo-jet engine whirled into life and the car took off at great speed from the almost deserted autobahn. It circled the baffled bishop once and then climbed rapidly into the calm, cloudless sky of the autumn afternoon.

A little later Jerry dropped altitude as he made out the impressive steeples of Cologne Cathedral. He checked his map and then began to descend towards the road that would take him to Nibelburg. To the west he thought he could just see the tall, stone tower where Dr Karen von Krupp lived, worked and schemed for the destruction of the organization and all it stood for.

The car touched down on the highway; its wings and tail section were retracted and it whipped along the concrete road until Jerry saw the sign saying he was about to enter Nibelburg.

Nibelburg was a few two- or three-storeyed houses and shops of grey and red brick, a little railway station, a larger police station with a great many motor-bikes parked outside it, and a church which had recently been converted into a dance hall.

Over the tops of the elms and poplars lining the fields beyond Nibelburg, Cornelius made out the tower he had seen from the air. He decelerated, began to whistle the *Chant d'amour* from the recently-finished symphony, and consulted his guide. The tower was reached by an unmade road about half a mile out of Nibelburg.

He stopped just before he came to the road, and he concentrated his attention on his mouth until he had a passable ache in one of his left molars. Feeling unhappy, he restarted the engine and turned into the side road, ignoring the Black Rat sign and bumping along for a quarter of a mile until he stopped outside the seventy-foot tower with its Gothic doorway, windows and battlements high above. The stone, which seemed to date from the earliest Gothic period, was extremely clean, with hardly a trace of a stain of any kind. It was pitted with age, and worn, especially around the lower parts of the wall, but nonetheless it was as well-scrubbed and looked after as a carefully kept tooth. Cornelius wondered if he climbed to the battlements he would find they had been filled with amalgam or even gold.

He parked the car neatly at the side of the tower. Only one other car was there, a Volkswagen sports, which, he gathered, belonged to the doctor.

He walked up the gravel path and raised the heavy iron door-knocker, letting it fall with a thump that fled away into the tower's interior.

The door was opened almost instantly by a beautiful blonde girl of about sixteen. She had blue eyes of a largeness that was accentuated by her use of mascara. There was a smile on her wide, full mouth; her hair was long and straight, covering the back and shoulders of a short-skirted dress of rich white brocade that was probably a Biba copy. She wore matching brocade tights and Granny shoes. Her arms were almost entirely bare and her skin was as sweet and soft as the silk of Jerry's suit, the colour of the first warm streaks of a spring sunrise.

'*Ja?*' she said, a depraved look appearing momentarily in her eyes.

'Do you speak English,' said Jerry lazily, 'Southern English?'

'*Ja*, of course.' She looked him over slowly and with a certain amount of awakening surprise, as if she had not at first been struck by his black skin and his turban. What had been her first impression? Jerry wondered.

Cornelius put his hand to his cheek. 'I was going through Nibelburg,' he told the girl, 'when I was overcome with toothache. I enquired at the police station and they told me that I would find a dentist here.'

'And more,' said the girl mysteriously, standing aside to let him enter and gesturing vaguely with the dildo in her left hand.

When he stood in the polished oak hall, she closed the door with a crash and popped the dildo into the umbrella stand, folding her hands under her breasts and looking down at the floor.

'You wish to see Doctor von Krupp?' she said at length.

'I believe that is the name I was given.'

The girl raised her perfect eyebrows. 'But your first name?'

'It's Michael,' he said. 'I call myself Mike.'

'This way.' She began to walk along the hall, paused at the stone, oak-banister stairway until he had caught up with her, and then began to ascend.

On the fourth landing, the girl stopped and knocked gently at the only door. A voice came from the other side. Jerry couldn't hear the words. The girl turned the handle and they wandered in together, into a high-ceilinged surgery with a large window of rich, stained glass – a pastoral scene from the sixteenth century. The glass was exquisite and Jerry stared at it for several seconds before he saw the luxurious dentist's chair, the chrome-finished instrument stand, the dentist, at a desk in one corner, looking through a stack of index cards.

'Herr Michael von Krupp,' said the girl gently. 'A toothache.'

'Aserinsky,' said Jerry.

Doctor von Krupp smiled condescendingly and spoke in German: 'You must leave, *liebchen*.' The girl glanced through narrowed eyes at Jerry and then went out.

Dr Karen von Krupp was about thirty in a stiff, black and white paisley overall, black net stockings and purple charley boots. Her hair was a deep, dark red, very thick and wavy, worn at shoulder length. Her face was strong, with pronounced cheek-bones, intelligent and attractive. Her lipstick almost matched her shoes and her eyebrows were pencilled thin to match her hair. She spread back her overall to put her hands on her hips and revealed a dress of layered chiffon that was predominantly bottle-green, its hem six inches above the knees of her long, well-shaped legs. Her taste, thought Jerry, was dreadful, but splendid.

'It is Herr Michael Aserinsky?' the woman asked, smiling once.

'It is.' He admired her figure. 'A toothache.'

'*Ja, ja.*' She turned and began to pack the index cards into a box on the desk. Jerry took off his coat.

'Will you go and sit in the chair, please.'

'Well.' Jerry wondered why he was here.

'And remove your – *hat*,' she said firmly, then laughed.

'No,' he said.

'But you must.' She looked over her shoulder, staring hard, smiling again. 'Otherwise, you see, I cannot get a proper grip on you.'

'My political convictions . . .'

'You have some?'

'Forbid me, doctor, from removing my turban in the presence of a woman. I hadn't realized . . .'

'Ah,' she closed the lid of the box, 'So,' began buttoning up her overall. 'Still, Herr Aserinsky, you must decide whether you would feel in health in this world or suffer a moment or two somewhere else.'

Jerry's hand began to move towards his vibragun, but he stopped it with great self-control. 'Perhaps you could first look at the tooth and tell me what you think needs work. Then we can decide.'

'But you could be making me waste my time.' She shrugged. 'Very well, into the chair, sir.'

He clambered warily into the chair and rested his head back so that he was looking at the upper part of the stained glass window and a section of the drilling rig.

'You like my window?' She picked up a barbed tool from the tray of instruments. 'Open wide, please,' and she began to poke and scrape at his teeth. 'What do you think about cocaine?'

He blinked.

When she stepped back she was smiling. 'Black teeth. Like black marble. Curious.'

'You noticed?' He tried to rise. 'The pain's gone now. Psychosomatic, I suppose.'

'You're an expert at that, aren't you?'

'Um,' he said.

'Why have you got black teeth, then? Painted with white enamel by the look of it . . .'

'Bored with them . . .'

'I think not. Re-born, perhaps.'

Jerry's hand fled into his jacket and grasped the butt of the vibragun. 'Dancing was never more disgusting than when done by Kelly, eh?'

'I'm with you there.'

He felt sick. He poised himself to jump from the chair, noticing how beautiful she was. He fell in love with her.

'Why did you come here?' She replaced the hooked instrument on the tray and looked down into his eyes. She did something to the chair and he was tilted back even farther. His fingers fell limply from the gun-butt. Her face came closer, the lips opening to show large, even teeth (two of them gold) and a huge, curling tongue.

He dropped his hand away from the gun altogether. It went out, instead, to grasp her thigh, feeling the ridge of a suspender belt beneath the thin material of dress and overall.

She kissed him coarsely.

'Oh,' he said. He still felt sick. He was breathing heavily.

'Ah,' he said as she drew back. 'Who cares?'

An unpleasant whine from outside. The blonde girl came in. 'Rockets,' she said.

There was a crash from below.

'No warheads,' said Jerry, getting up, drawing his gun and putting his arm around Karen von Krupp's shoulders. 'Pack a bag, doctor.' He pulled on his coat.

'That's real Panda, isn't it?' she asked, fingering it. 'Where did it come from – Moscow or London?'

Another rocket whined in and grazed the roof.

'Ouch,' she said. 'Perhaps my husband . . .'

'Pack a bag. We'll go to Paris.'

'Wait a moment, then.'

2. Presidents in Parade Scandal!

'Time flies,' said Jerry.

'And who, these days, knows his name?' smiled Karen von Krupp tenderly as the crystal city became distinct ahead.

Left fingertips on her knee, right on the wheel, Jerry cruised at ninety towards Paris. 'There is something,' he said, 'concerning Russia. But what about America?'

'I don't know what you mean, darling.' She drew on her long cigarette holder one last puff and threw the whole contraption from the window. 'Well, that's over.'

'Something's going on,' he said.

'Always. And was it not you, anyway, who engineered the Moscow thing?'

'Possibly,' said Jerry, frowning desperately, glancing behind him at the blonde girl who, pouting disinterestedly, lounged in the back seats. 'You'd better change into an ankle-length skirt. You know what they're like in the Three Republics about that sort of thing.' He touched a stud and the glass partition slid down, allowing her to crawl into the back of the car. The blonde girl moved over and looked out of the window.

While she changed he looked at his map for the best route into Paris.

In the rearview mirror he noticed that Bishop Beesley had caught up with him again for there was the silver Cadillac spinning along behind them, a fat, pasty figure at the wheel. Jerry blacked out the back windows.

'That's clever,' she said, struggling into a long, bottle-green skirt. He wondered if all her skirts were bottle-green and all her shoes purple. It indicated an interest in Ouspensky, at very least.

In Paris they were just in time to watch the presidents ride by, their white horses wading, sometimes swimming, through the watery streets, sending up a fine, bright spray in the pale sunshine.

Along the Champs-Elysées the procession made its way, some

of it on foot, some in barges, some in carriages, some on horse-back.

As best they could the presidents waved to the few soaked spectators (survivors of the plague) who shivered on both sides of the wide street, knee-deep in water. The presidents led the Three Republics of France, Spain and Portugal (there had been four before the Israeli annexation of Greece) who had resisted offers from the US wanting to send in some advisors.

Old age had made the presidents almost identical, with the same vacant eyes, drooling mouths, yellow, wrinkled skins and near-hairless heads. They were strapped firmly to horses almost as old as themselves. They were said to be very sentimentally attached to their horses.

A little behind them laboured the band; each musician up to his waist in water. The bass drums were muffled and every time the drummers struck a beat they sent a fountain of water into their own faces. There was water in all the brass, but they marched resolutely against the current, playing a burbling *La Marseillaise.*

'Touching,' said Karen von Krupp stroking his leg.

Jerry leaned back in the moored Phantom VI, his arm comfortably around Dr van Krupp's shoulders. She smiled and the car rocked gently in the wake of the presidential passing.

'Shall we go to the Assembly and hear the speeches?' She glanced back at the blonde girl. Jerry shook his head.

He cast off and began to turn the car into the current.

There was a tabac on his right and Jerry looked at it nervously as he went past. Someone was peering at him from the first floor window. He recognized the thin, intense nose.

It was Pyat, chief of the organization's Moscow agency and a Chekist. What was he doing in Paris? Jerry pretended he hadn't seen him and pulled the car's throttle full out, boiling down the Champs-Elysécs as fast as he could go.

Behind him ploughed Bishop Beesley's silver Cadillac, hood barely above the water.

'Ubiquitous,' Jerry murmured and stopped outside the Hotel Aspiration. 'Hurry, my dear, before he turns the corner. Leap,' he said, opening the door, 'to the step there. I'll bring our bags in later.'

Dr von Krupp leapt. The blonde girl leapt after her. Jerry

his wash slapping against windows on both sides. But Beesley was in too deep water and had given up the chase. Soon Cornelius was able to return, moor the car in the hotel's garage, and join his love in the lobby.

'It's just a front,' he said, pressing a bell on the reception desk. The floor fell away with them, bearing them deep into the ground.

'Underground,' he told her, indicating the musty darkness. 'Safe and sound.'

'A trap,' she said.

'Not so.'

As the section of the floor rose back to join the rest, he switched on lights and green brilliance filled the room. She studied the lust in his face.

'I must be careful,' she said. 'My husband ...' Then she yelled with excitement as he fell upon her.

'It has been too much for me,' he growled, 'today.'

And they rolled about all over the Dunlopillo flooring while the blonde girl sat in the corner looking on with boredom.

3. Transvestite Orgy in Paris Hotel

'Husbands and wives, sisters and brothers, mothers and sons,' said Bishop Beesley, adjusting his mitre and grinning at Jerry who was spreadeagled against the wall. Karen von Krupp, wearing an ermine-trimmed cape of red velvet and an elaborate crown, crossed her legs and leaned back moodily in her throne. Bishop Beesley reached out with his crook and pushed up Jerry's skirt, tickling the balls that bulged in the black lace knickers they had dressed him in while he was unconscious. 'White pubic hair. I hadn't expected that, Mr Aserinsky.'

'And I hadn't expected this, bishop.'

'Well, well – you can't just go around committing adultery like that and expect to get away with it, can you? There's some decency left in the world, I hope.'

'So, what's your plan?'

'A restoration. For your own good. Actually, I bear you no malice.'

'My name isn't –'

'Aserinsky. So you say.'

'It's Jerry Cornelius.'

'So you say.'

Someone moved in the shadows and began to wade across the Dunlopillo. It was Pyat, his dark face concerned.

'It's Alan Powys, isn't it?' said Pyat.

'So you say,' said Jerry.

'Mitzi!' Bishop Beesley snapped his fingers as best he could. 'This is getting to be a drag. Use the machines for heaven's sake,' murmured Karen von Krupp.

'I hate artificial methods,' said Jerry.

'Connie Nuttall.'

'Colvin,' said Jerry. 'Connie Colvin. Tragic wasn't it?'

'What's in a name?' The blonde girl appeared. She had hoisted up her dress and was strapping on a black dildo.

'Fuck that,' said Bishop Beesley. 'I do apologize.' The blonde girl began to bugger him.

Jerry glanced at Karen von Krupp, but she looked away. He was dressed in the full set: curly red wig, make-up, white lace blouse, falsies, girdle, suspender-belt, fishnet stockings, high-heels, a tight, black skirt.

Bishop Beesley's head was close to the floor and his shout was muffled. 'Don't worry, sir. We'll soon have everything back to normal. You'll feel a new person once this is over!'

'How did you get down here?' Jerry asked Karen von Krupp.

'They followed you. Pyat pressed the button.'

'Somebody has to,' said Pyat.

'You got the dope while you slept.'

'I thought you were on my side,' Jerry said to Pyat.

'I am. You'll realize that one day.'

'I don't fancy this. It's like something out of the political age.'

'Not all of us have your faith in the future, Comrade Cornelius.'

'Well, there's no time like the present.'

Pyat pulled down his pants. 'That'll have to be dealt with.'

He turned to Karen von Krupp. 'You're a surgeon, aren't you? Could you do it?'

She shrugged. 'I've done it before.'

The bishop rose from his hands and knees. 'Now, let me see.'

Jerry wondered if he were losing his patience. 'Bishop – I don't know whether you realize ...'

'I understand. I understand. This is your home and we were not invited. But these are troubled times, my dear. Needs must, as it were.'

'Mitzi,' said Karen von Krupp.

The blonde girl stepped forward.

'Snap the staples off. Let our friend join us.'

Mitzi freed Jerry.

The bishop glanced curiously at Karen von Krupp. 'You want to ... ? A party?'

'Why not?'

A strobe began to flash and the room filled with sound. It was Jimi Hendrix's *Voodoo Child* distorted because of the volume, but they couldn't be expected to know that, particularly since they were reeling about. Jerry strode through the strobe-light and took Karen von Krupp by the arm. She was vomiting spasmodically. He saw his clothes in a corner with his gun on top. There was only time to get the gun and aim it at the wall.

'Cheer up,' he told her. 'It's going to be worse before it's better. This is a bit of an emergency.'

'Where are we going?'

'Through the Shift. I always keep one handy.'

The wall fell away and Jerry hefted up his skirt and stuck the gun in his girdle.

Somewhere a mammoth screamed.

4. Our Night of Horror

Around them the air was jewelled and faceted, glistening and alive with myriad colours, flashing, scintillating, swirling and beautiful. She clung to him. 'What is it?'

'The multiverse. All layers of existence seen at once. Get it?'

'Philosophy isn't my bent.'

'This is physics, dear. Get in.'

'Where are we?'

'Ah, that's the chance you have to take. Keep walking.'

The air cleared. They stood on a green plain close to a clump of oaks. In the shade of the oaks stood a small man with a goatee and rimless glasses. He had a large black metal box under his arm.

'Would you believe it?' Jerry said with some excitement. 'The bugger's got it.'

'That looks like ...'

'That's right. Good old comrade ... Hey!' Jerry began to run towards him, hampered by Karen von Krupp, who refused to let go of his arm, and by the tight skirt and high heels.

A wave of jewels without substance washed over them. 'My machine!' shouted Jerry and his voice echoed for a long time. 'Oh, well. Some other time. I thought it was too good to be true.'

'What machine?'

'That'd be telling. Unless you already know. I suspect Bishop Beesley does know and that's what he's after – ultimately speaking, at any rate.'

They were now walking through the streets of St Petersburg in the early morning. It was very romantic. Jerry pointed out the little cluster of figures staring at them from the top of an office block in Bronstein Prospekt. '*Homo habilis* by the look of them. Funny little sods, aren't they?'

Down the middle of the prospekt galloped a brontotherium herd. They dashed into a canal.

'It's very quiet,' she said.

'Yes, it would be.'

'What's the time?'

'Not sure. Post-political, I'd say. But you can never be sure. This could be a complete mix-up. I wish I had a fix.'

Bishop Beesley confronted them, threatening them with some sort of insect spray.

'We know all about you, my dear Mr Cornelius,' he said. 'You and your women friends. Oh, God, it's disgusting! This *is* 1970! You're so primitive!'

'You think I should feel guilty?' Jerry got a grip on his vibragun. You could never be sure.

'I think someone should, dear.'

'Where can we talk?'

The bishop bent down and picked up his attaché case, tucking his equipment inside. Then he held the case to his chest with all the affection an old woman might give to her parrot.

'I've got a marvellous little latty here,' he said. 'Taste! You've never seen the like.'

'Sounds sweet. But this'll do.'

The three of them sat down at the sidewalk table, under the big umbrella. A surly waiter took their order.

'It's time to make up, Mr Cornelius,' said the bishop. 'I've such a horror of tension. I can't bear it.'

'Not yet, bishop.'

'But this is *Denmark*. So *neutral*.'

'I see I've caught you at a weak moment.' Jerry got up. 'Come on, Karen. I'll be seeing you, bishop.'

'Cruelty! The world is full of cruelty!' The bishop tucked into their strudels.

They strolled on through the multiverse. 'Where did he come from?' she said. 'What was the conversation about?'

'What are conversations ever about? He seemed to know. Doubtless we'll meet again, either before or after, or not at all. Keep walking.'

'The sooner we get back to the sane world, the better,' she said waspishly.

'You're just sore because you didn't get your coffee.'

They were walking on concrete. Ahead of them was the huge silhouette of a Lockheed SR-72 Mach 3 two-seat interceptor and strategic reconnaissance aircraft framed against the dawn. 'Would you believe it? Maybe it's something you said.'

'I feel funny.'

'You probably do. It's all magic, really. We're out of the tunnel – or nearly. Run.'

They tripped on their high heels until they reached the aircraft. 'Hop in,' he said. 'I think you must have a talent, Fraulein Doktor.'

'Do you know how to fly these monsters?'

'Oh, come off it.'

5. Fly Your Eggs Right Down Their Stacks!

'I've had very little private life since all this started,' explained Jerry as they took off from Orly airport and were momentarily pursued by some Starfighters that fell to pieces behind them. He spoke through the intercom. 'You look beautiful in that helmet.' He guided the plane towards the Channel.

'Thank you.' She put her hand on the portion of his thigh that was bare between his stocking and suspender belt. He decelerated.

'I don't want to fly at maximum speed,' he explained, 'because I've got eight AIM-174s to get rid of and they're not really suitable for the job I've got in mind.'

She accepted his apology with a polite little smile.

The 95 ft aircraft soon reached the Channel and flak began to appear as the pirates tried to hit it. Jerry angled the plane towards them, hoping for the best, and released all the air-to-air missiles in rapid succession. There were a few explosions, then they had passed the ships and were circling off the coast. 'Stand by to eject,' he said and putting the plane into a steep dive yanked the ejector lever.

They drifted down towards the cliffs. He leaned over and kissed her. Water gouted as the plane hit the sea.

They landed gently and got out.

'You don't look too jolly, Herr C,' she remarked.

'Light or square, I suppose it's all the same to me, Doktor Krupp.' He smoothed his skirt. 'Well, that wasn't too bad, was it? Sure the velocity didn't bother you?'

'It's something you get used to.'

'Of course you do.' He squeezed her hand affectionately.

Result

'In every war in history there must have been a considerable flow of genes one way or another. Whether the genes of the victors or of the vanquished have increased most is a debatable point.'

Papazian, *Modern Genetics*

1. America Takes 'No Nonsense' Line

Curled in deep leather armchairs beside a comfortable fire in the sitting room of Jerry's Ladbroke Grove HQ Jerry and Karen von Krupp listened to Groucho Marx singing *Father's Day* while they caught up with the newspapers.

It seemed that Israel, having annexed Turkey, Greece and Bulgaria, was putting it about that Rumania and Albania were threatening her security. US President Teddy 'Angel Face' Paolozzi had increased the number of military advisors sent to Europe to three million. They were under the command of General Ulysses Washington Cumberland whose mission was to keep order in Europe and seek out 'certain fifth column elements.' The British parliament, both government and opposition, had been arrested as their jumbo Trident was about to take off for Gibraltar. President Paolozzi had sent a diplomatic note to Israel that read *Stay off of our turf, Israel, or else.* A riot in Prague had received universal censure from the European press. 'Uncool' was the *Daily Mirror* verdict. Bubonic plague remained unchecked in Berlin and Lübeck.

Jerry stopped reading. Evidently, there was little news of any relevance.

'What now?' said Karen von Krupp as Jerry took her hand and pulled her down to the rug. He tore off her clothes, tore off his own knickers and made fierce love to her. Again and again she came and when he fell back, his wig askew, his skirt torn and his stockings laddered, she sighed. 'Ach! At last – a man who is a man!'

2. His Choice: Die Now or Rot Tomorrow!

Jerry looked past the bars and glass of the window at the houses in the street beyond the wall. Grey rain fell. Through the rain ran a pack of girls, few over five feet, with narrow, stooped shoulders and cheap see-through blouses and tight little skirts stretched over thick thighs. He sighed. Ukrainian Nationalist guerillas.

The Animals, The Who, Zoot Money's Big Roll Band, The Spencer Davis Group, The Moody Blues, Georgie Fame and the Blue Flames, Geno Washington and the Ram Jam Band, Chris Farlowe and the Thunderbirds, The Steam Packet, Manfred Mann, Jesus Christ and the Apostles. Where were the groups of yesterday?

Behind him, Karen von Krupp listened moodily to Ives's *Symphony No 1 in D Minor*. He wondered if that wasn't the key to the whole thing.

'Still here,' he said.

She nodded.

'There's something on your mind,' she murmured.

'Something indigestible. I've been too long in the wilderness, honey.'

'Don't say that, Jerry.'

'I've got to face it.'

'You can make it.'

'Sure. I can make it.'

'Are all your relatives dead now?'

'I sometimes think they must be. My mother ...'

'What are you going to do?'

'I'll decide soon. The world is ruled by bad poets. I must do something about it.'

'That's your mission?'

'More or less, honey. More or less.'

'Are you asking or telling?'

'Mothers can't die, can they?'

3. My Deadly Mission

'It's a question of polarities,' he told her as they slid about in the bed. 'A problem of equilibrium.'

   'I told you. I don't understand philosophy.'

   'I told you. This is physics.'

   'What will become of you?'

   'I'll probably die. I almost always do.'

   'Don't die on me, *liebchen.*'

   'A lot depends on the next movement.'

   'Denn wovon lebt der Mensch?'

   'Maybe. It's all a *dreckhaufen* really.'

   'Isn't that the way you like it?'

   'Sure.'

   'You'll never die.'

   'Not in that sense, of course. Still, it gets boring.'

   'Then why don't you stop?'

   'Ich möchte auch mal was Schönes sehen ...'

4. Sing High, Sweetie – For Tonight You Fry!

His brain cleared. The process took a few minutes.

From somewhere there came a faint hissing sound. 'My programme,' he murmured, smiling back in the darkness. 'Mo?'

5. Amnesia: Why You Get It

An early postcard showing Loch Promenade, Douglas, Isle of Man, with a single-deck open-sided omnibus drawn by a horse. The people wear Edwardian clothes. The tower clock in the foreground says 11.22. The card is post-marked Liverpool, May 31st 1968. The message and address are partially obscured – 'We may arrive Sunday anyway see you soon! Una pp JRC.' *79 Tavistock Road, London, W11.*

6. What was Secret of 'Thing in the Cellar'?

It was a machine of intense beauty consisting of delicate red, gold and silver webs, strands of which brushed his face and had the vital warmth of human skin.

The webs rustled as he entered them, and they began to sing. He relaxed. Beesley's plan had almost worked and the Shift, in this instance, hadn't really helped, either. Still, the machine would set all that right. They certainly needed each other.

Refreshed, sobered, he contemplated the possibilities.

2. EMERGENCY OPERATION

shooting games are provided the year round.

GOVERNMENT EQUIPMENT SALES.
NRA members are eligible to purchase from the Army, such firearms as are declared surplus from time to time. Spare parts and targets are also available.

FIREARMS LEGISLATIVE SERVICE.
NRA members receive monthly gun legislation information through the *American Rifleman*. Bills requiring emergency action are reported to members concerned through special bulletins.

YOU CAN BE PROUD TO BELONG.
NRA is the largest, oldest organization of sportsmen devoted to preserving your right to keep and use firearms for lawful purposes. More than 800,000 hunters and shooters enjoy NRA's many benefits.

Ad, *Guns & Ammo* magazine

Anaesthetic

'Along with the Smothers Brothers and Rowan and Martin, (Mort Sahl) is part of that radical fringe who try to tear down American decency and democracy.'

Howard Miller, WCFL, Chicago

1. Lynda Bird to Wed George Hamilton?

The next day Jerry and Karen went to the pictures. They sat in the front seats of the Circle and ate popcorn as they watched *Drums Along the Mersey*. Sir William Harrison played the moody, introverted explorer, Ina Shorrock was the proud Queen of Port Sunlight and Eric Bentcliffe emerged in one of his best roles as the rascally trader from the interior.

2. My Teenage Wife Won't Let Me Out of Her Sight

Leaving the cinema they walked hand in hand down Westbourne Grove in the late sunshine. A West Indian with a tray around his neck sold Jerry a pot of Chaulmoogra, guaranteed as treatment for leprosy.

A squadron of M-60 tanks, mounted on guarded flat-cars, went past them towards Queensway. A crowd of dancing children followed the tanks. The grinning soldiers threw Hershey Bars and Tootsie Rolls to the children.

'Flash' Gordon Gavin was seen, walking rapidly towards the nearest tank.

3. How a Banana Endangers the Lennon Sisters

Jerry signalled for the gate of his Ladbroke Grove HQ to be opened. A Corporation Dustcart turned the corner.

Balanced on the cab was a man in a fur jacket and a fez. His right hand clung to the truck's canopy and he shouted vigorously through a megaphone.

'Bring out your dead! Bring out your dead!'

It was Mo Collier, collecting for charity again.

4. Why Connie Threatened Eddie with a Lawyer

Jerry poured himself a Pernod and handed the glass of Tio Pepe to Karen von Krupp. They were dressed in identical velvet suits of violent violet from Mr Fish. The effect was a little more pleasing than a Pre-Raphaelite painting. Their flies were undone.

5. The Secret Mia Won't Tell Frank

They lay naked on the red plush bed cover staring up at the blue plush canopy of the brass four poster. Their skins, black and pink, shone with health.

'Fresh air,' he said. 'That's it.'

'Why?'

'It'll be necessary to go to the country sooner or later. We've been in London a fortnight, you know.'

'And nothing's happened. Are you worried by the stillness?'

'I suppose so. There's a shipment tomorrow. It could go straight out again.' He sniffed at her hair.

She began to stroke the skin of his inner thigh.

'It's too good to be true.' She nipped his forearm with her teeth.

First Incision

Newly and/or unexpectedly imposed tyranny can make people commit suicide.

Tomáš Masaryk

1. How Much Longer Can This Last ? ? ? ?

Having left one Phantom VI in Paris, Jerry didn't feel up t using another. Besides, he was in no hurry. 'We'll go by rive I think.'

He drew his vibragun and went upstairs.

When he next passed the door he was herding a group c sullen transmog patients in front of him. They all wore strai waistcoats and most of them would have looked handsome c pretty if they had been able to manage a smile or two. Kare von Krupp patted her hair.

Jerry reassured her as they reached the cool main hal 'They'll soon be laughing on the other side of their faces.'

It was a lovely day.

Waiting in the courtyard was a white hovertruck with re crosses painted on its sides. When he'd stowed the passenge comfortably at the back Jerry joined Karen in the cockpit an started the engines. Whining, they lifted up and began to mov forward through the open gates.

Soon they were whistling down the road, passed the scarl gloom of Chelsea, and reached the Thames Embankment. 'O it is *wunderbar*!' Karen von Krupp looked out at the wrec of the tankers poking up through oil that shone with dozens (bright colours.

'You can't beat it,' Jerry agreed affectionately.

They crossed Waterloo Bridge with the siren going and we waved through by a Marine with a sensitive earnest face wl leaned one hand on the butt of his Navy Colt and held a cig in the other. The white hovertruck sang onwards into tl ruined roads of South London that were full of colombin ragged robin, foxglove, golden rain, dog rose, danewort, iv creeping cinquefoil, Venus's Comb, deadnettle, shepherc purse and dandelion, then turned towards Greenwich whe Jerry's cruiser, *The Pierrot*, was moored.

As Jerry directed his patients up the gangplank Karen v

Krupp pointed to a battered, broken-looking building in the distance. 'What is that, Jerry?'

'Greenwich Observatory,' he said. 'It's a bit redundant now, I suppose.'

She came aboard and he cast off.

In a moment they were chugging away from London, moving strongly against the current.

The banks of the river and the fields and ruins beyond them were carpeted with flowers of every description. While Jerry switched the boat over to automatic steering, Karen stretched out on the deck, breathing the warm summer air, staring up at the deep blue sky and listening to the bees and the crickets on the shore.

When they were sailing through a forest of oaks and elms Jerry came and lay down beside her. From the cabin came the faint strains of Ives's *Symphony No 1*.

'That is a favourite of yours, I would say,' she said.

'In a manner of speaking.'

'This is the life, is it not?'

'Which?'

'Which do you like?'

'Oh, all of them really.'

The prow pushed on through the rainbow oil and every so often a quaintly-shaped fish would leap out and rest on the surface until the ripples opened the top up and it would fall back under again.

The river turned out of the forest and they sailed between fields and old, ruined farmhouses, deserted villages and abandoned pubs. Once, as they moved under a bridge, an armoured car roared over their heads and moaned off down the road. A little later a scrawny young woman threw stones at them from the bank and screamed incoherent insults. Jerry caught a few words. *'Pantalones – el jardin zoologico – la iglesia inglesa! Lavabo – negra – queremos un – vino dulce – de oro, plata, platino, diamantes, rubies, zafiros, esmeraldas, perlas ...'*

'American immigrant, poor cow.'

Karen cocked her head, brushing back her long red hair. 'What was that? Not bees.'

The woman had disappeared into the undergrowth.

Jerry listened.

'Hornets?' Karen suggested.

Jerry shook his head. 'Westland Whirlwinds. I'd better just ...' He jumped and ran to the bridge. Karen got up and then fell over on her bottom as a small missile launcher purred from the forward hatch. She crawled to the bridge. He was watching the radar.

'About eight of them,' he said. 'Hard to say whose they are.' He peered through the window. 'They've seen us. They're coming to take a closer look.'

'Are they ours, Jerry?'

'No, I think they're yours. Perhaps your husband ...'

'My husband?'

'Maybe.'

Jerry switched on the laservision and tuned it to the radar. Now he had a close-up of the leading Whirlwind and its pilot.

The pilot was thoughtfully chewing through a chocolate layer cake as he stared down at Jerry's boat.

'I wonder where he's been,' Jerry's hand went to the launcher's controls. 'I wouldn't like to hurt him.'

'Does he know this is your boat?'

'I shouldn't think so. It's registered in the name of Beesley.'

'A peculiar coincidence.'

'What's peculiar about it?'

But now the helicopters had spotted the launcher and, even though equipped with superior Nord SS 11 air-to-surface missiles, began to bank away.

'*Velocidad maxima*, I think ...' Jerry murmured.

'What?'

'The sloop. Time to be on the move.'

'Saints ...'

The helicopters vanished over the horizon.

'They're heading for London,' she said. 'I think we got away just in time.'

'You could be right.'

'Do you think I'm wrong?'

'Well, they weren't carrying their full complement of missiles but they were lying rather heavy on the air, wouldn't you say?' He depressed a button and his own launcher disappeared into the bowels of the boat.

2. It's a Fad, Dad!

Jerry took over the steering as they turned into the Urzel tributary and moved slowly along beneath a canopy of tall aromatic grass. It was evening now and the sun was low, but a little light filtered through to them.

Since the departure of the helicopters, Karen von Krupp had become introspective and had stayed beside him in the cabin, repeatedly playing the Ives piece. Something was bothering her. Finally, as they approached a wooden landing stage, she said, 'Is this, do you think, the answer to our relationship?'

'Of course not.' He squeezed her hand and steered the boat in. 'It's merely the key to the future. Possibly not even that. Don't worry about it.'

With a pout she took the mooring line and jumped to the landing stage, winding the line round and round the oak capstan as he guided the boat into its position. He cut the engines.

'Now let's get those lubbers ashore.' Drawing his vibragun he kicked open the stern hatch. 'All right, mates, out you come. Slowly now.'

Blinking in the last of the sunlight, the transmog patients stumbled on deck and trooped down the gangplank that Karen von Krupp had erected for them.

They all set off along the landing stage towards a field of corn.

'Have you ever wondered about the morality of what you are doing?' she asked. 'These creatures never asked ...'

'They prayed. We heard. We merely serve the people, Karen.'

'Beesley says...'

'... he does, too. I know. Beesley knows what's good for them. I simply do what they want me to do. There it is. I'm all for equilibrium.'

They walked along a small path through the corn. A rabbit ran away from them and a partridge whirled into the sky. The roof of a large house could now be seen in the distance. It was Sunnydale Reclamation Centre. Welcoming smoke rose from

the chimneys. 'Not much farther now,' Jerry told the transmog
patients who tramped ahead, looking at the ground.

'You never question ...'

'What is there to question?'

'I ...'

'I do what they want me to do.'

'It's like prostitution.'

'It's a lot like prostitution, isn't it?'

'You see nothing wrong ... ?'

'The customer's always right.'

'And you have no,' she shuddered, 'ethics?'

'I give the public what it wants, if that's what you mean.'

'You have no sense of mission! Ach! At least Beesley has
that!' She laughed harshly. 'Ha!'

'I thought it was the same as mine.'

'*Nein*. It is different. He knows that people want a sense of
security.'

'Of course. Do you smell burning?'

'*Ja*, I do.'

3. The Erotic Ghosts of Viet Nam

Sunnydale was burning. The staff stood about in the grounds staring helplessly at the Reclamation Centre. Incendiary rockets had done their worst.

'What about the patients?' Jerry asked Matron.

'All gone, Doctor Finlay. Kidnapped. Months of work! Och...'

'Calm yourself, woman,' said Jerry with gruff kindness. 'Was it the Westland Whirlwinds?'

'Aye, doctor. Eight Mark Tens. We didna have a chance tae activate the defences. We lased London. Mister Koutrouboussis is on his way. He said he'd try tae bring ye with him.'

'I'm ahead of him. Is the laser still working?'

'Noo...'

'Then you'd better get off to Soho as fast as you can, Janet. Tell them the choppers were heading for London when last seen.'

'Aye, doctor.' Matron ran for the one hangar still intact. Soon a small OH-6A turbine-powered copter moaned upwards, its pilot hastily pulling on her American uniform to conform with the machine's markings. It flew away over the fields of flowers.

The sun set and the fire went down.

'The damage isn't too bad, considering,' said Mo, one of the male nurses, vainly trying to brush off the black patches on his smock with a limp hand. 'All the East wing is okay, Mr C.'

'They had these big bazookas and stuff,' said Fowles, the Transplant Chief. Fowles was a tall, pale man with unhealthy hands, a sweaty nature. 'We didn't stand a chance. We were rounded up, marked in this stuff,' he pointed to the blob of green paint on his forehead, 'and herded into the garden. Then they took away the patients.'

'Their leader ... ?' Jerry raised a finger to his nose.

'Dressed in clerical gear. He stole the birthday cake Matron had made for the ex-chairman of the Arts Council, the poor

cunt had lost so much weight!'

'You've had the cake, I'm afraid,' said Jerry, 'but I'll see if I can get the patients back. Miserable things. They must be in a state.'

'To say the least, sir.' Fowles tucked his hands under his arms. 'Timid little creatures at that stage, you know. Don't understand. Couldn't tell you their own names, half of them.'

'You'd better get this lot into the East wing.' Jerry indicated the new batch. Most of them had seated themselves on the ground and were staring moodily at the Centre's smoking skeleton. 'I'll be over at my place if you want me. Come on, Karen.'

He led her across the lawns to his little Dutch mansion and stopped under the carved portal.

'Open, als't u blieft!' The door swung open.

They stepped inside.

'Waar is de nooduitgang?' asked Karen absently as the door shut behind her. Jerry turned on the lights.

'You're getting very tense,' he said.

'Ik hank det wel ...'

'Sad ...'

'Ja, das i seben schade ...'

They walked along the hall. All the wood was dark and shiny with polish. A clean old man rounded a corner and tottered towards them. 'Ah, sir! Ah, sir!'

'What have we got to eat, "de Vossenberg"?'

'Gekookte eieren, kaas, fazant ...'

'Fine. We'll have it in the parlour, I think.'

The parlour had walls of the same dark, panelled wood. The armchairs were deep and old-fashioned, covered in loose folds of floral material. The room was full of clocks in painted wooden cases, each keeping perfect time.

They sat in the chairs and said nothing.

After a while 'de Vossenberg' wheeled in the dumb waiter. 'Ah, sir.'

He gave them trays then he gave them plates then he served them with cold pheasant, cheese and boiled eggs. Then he opened a bottle of Niersteiner and poured it into two long-stemmed Czech hock glasses.

'What is going to happen now?' asked Karen von Krupp. 'You have lost most of your victims.'

'I suppose we should try to get them back.'

'Your duty?'

'Well ...'

'But Beesley will take them to Amerika!'

'How do you know?'

'I just think he would.'

'He told you.'

'No.'

'You knew.'

'Ja ...'

'Losing – lost – gone ... Now it makes sense.'

There was a knock at the front door. They heard 'de Vossenberg' shuffle to answer it. They heard voices.

'Koutrouboussis,' said Jerry as the Greek, sour-faced, entered the room and glanced disdainfully at the food. 'A bite?'

'A fish, eh?'

'No, a mistress. Doktor von Krupp and I are together now.'

'I'm getting suspicious of you, Cornelius.'

'No need, Mr Koutrouboussis. I'll be off to the States shortly.'

'You heard about the converted Concorde, then? All we got from Beesley was the bang. We've a responsibility to those poor bloaters, Cornelius. You must get them back. They're neither fish, nor fowl, nor good red herring as they are.'

'We'll leave in an hour or two.'

'Immediately.'

'We've got to book seats, Mr Koutrouboussis. That's a civilized country. You can't just go sailing in there in one of your own planes. It would cause a scene. We'll have to take a scheduled flight.'

Koutrouboussis accepted this. 'There's a Pan Am airbus leaving in the morning or a VC 10 charter taking off at midnight from Gatwick. It's one of those refugee flights, but we could get you on it.'

'Karen will be with me.'

Koutrouboussis darted Jerry a tortured look. 'Okay. I'll arrange the booking for both of you. You'll have to travel as a monk and a nun.'

'Naturally. I've got the necessary gear upstairs.'

'Things are becoming crucial, Jerry. I think. You know how crucial? If only you could get back that machine.'

'It means going into the Shift, almost certainly.'

'You haven't any other way of contacting him?'

'He's a hard man to get hold of. For God's sake – he doesn't even exist. It takes time to contact people like that.'

'I know. Keep trying. With that machine, we could achieve everything ...'

'Beesley's aware of that. He tried to get it off me in Paris. He's sure I have it.'

'You haven't ... ?'

'Oh, fuck ...'

'He thinks, then, that we're much more powerful than we actually are?'

'Sure.'

'I thought this bloody raid had a note of desperation! Oi moi! Oi moi!'

'Chin up, Mr Koutrouboussis. Keep fishing.'

'Look at the state of the nets!'

'But many other changes are beginning to affect *your* life and mine! These new trends concern us all! Student revolt in 20 countries – VIOLENCE exploding on college campuses (but *not* on our Ambassador College campuses). It's shocking, but some universities are beginning to allow unmarried men and women students to sleep together in college dormitories! Then look at this NEW phenomenon – rebellious Hippies lolling aimlessly about, taking to drugs and unbridled sex.

'Look at the unhappy marriages, the increasing divorce rate, the tragedy of juvenile delinquents. All about us racial strife, mass demonstrations, riots, VIOLENCE – MURDER! Men in the public eye assassinated! Add to all this the population explosion – the deterioration of our cities – the fear of nuclear WAR that could erase all humanity from the earth!

'These things are now striking close to YOUR life, and mine! You read of them in newspapers and magazines – you hear of them on radio, and see them on television. BUT *WHERE* DO *YOU* FIND THE *ANSWERS*! Where the *SOLUTIONS*?

'Not only news stories and magazine articles – but whole books have pictured and described these NEW problems of humanity. But The PLAIN TRUTH gives YOU UNDERSTANDING – makes plain the ANSWERS! Many see and describe WHAT is *WRONG* in the world – The PLAIN TRUTH gives you the CAUSES, explains the REAL MEANING, reveals the ANSWERS, tells HOW these problems will be solved!

'To KNOW what's happening in the world is important. *OTHERS* report the news. But it's FAR *MORE* IMPORTANT to understand what these happenings and changing conditions all around you REALLY *MEAN*! And WHERE they are taking us! And *WHAT* are the ANSWERS AND SOLUTIONS! That's why The PLAIN TRUTH is so different.

'The PLAIN TRUTH is UNIQUE among publications.

'To bring you a true perspective, sound understanding, and the right answers, The PLAIN TRUTH draws on sources and worldwide resources unique to it alone.'

Herbert W. Armstrong, Editor, The PLAIN TRUTH

1. I Died on the Operating Table

As the old VC 10 landed at long last at Kennedy, Jerry yawned and put down his champagne glass. They had been queuing for a landing space for two hours and it was dark again.

The red, blue and orange neon of the airport had all the richness of a late Walt Disney and everything was defined very sharply in the manner of Burne Hogarth. It was just right.

They disembarked with the Poor Clares and the Benedictines. Karen von Krupp looked lovely as a cool Mother Superior and Jerry was a slick abbot from a fashionable monastery.

Their passports showed Karen's occupation as Dental Surgeon and Jerry's as Heart Specialist, but then all clergy had been re-categorized.

The passport control officer flipped through Jerry's papers. 'It says here you're Caucasian, mister.'

'That's right.'

The officer pushed back his cap and held the passport out in front of his eyes in a theatrical manner. 'Well, your picture's okay . . .'

'I've been out East a long time.'

'Israel?'

'The Caucasus.'

'All right. I guess you refugees have got special priorities. I hope they know what they're doing.'

Jerry and Karen collected their baggage off the conveyor. They had identical expensive suitcases of black leather with gold clasps.

Customs men in smoothly styled uniforms waved them through. They joined the other nuns and monks who had gathered around a group of shallow-eyed men and women in grey woollen suits and gaberdine coats who shook their hands and welcomed them to America. The leader of the welcomers, a Mr Silver, had a tanned, tight face and all his buttons were done up. He spoke grimly.

'I'm sure you're all mighty tired, friends, and want to get some shuteye. We have reservations for you at a near-by hotel. Tomorrow we'll meet you and tell you where you're being assigned and how you're going to get there. Might I say how much we admire our British cousins. Follow me, please.'

They trooped after Mr Silver and his committee, crossed a metal bridge over the road that ran beside the air terminal and saw an eight storey building advertised in gold neon as the Hotel Nixon.

'It hardly seems fair,' murmured Karen. 'Kennedy got an airport and a bloody launching site.'

'They weren't expecting a run,' said Jerry reasonably.

They went through the swing doors and into the featureless lobby. Mr Silver stepped over to the checking-in desk and spoke to the clerk who handed him a sheet of paper and a bunch of keys.

'This way, friends.' Mr Silver led them to the elevators. 'We're all on the sixth floor. Keep together, please.'

Mr Silver entered the first elevator with eight of his charges. A middle-aged woman, Mrs Bronson, wearing a belted suit and no make-up save her very red lipstick, herded Jerry, Karen and six monks into the second elevator. Peering at her sheet she started to hand out the keys.

'You're 604, Father Abbot. 605, Brother Simon. 606, Brother Peter. 607, Brother Matthew. 608, Brother John. 609, Brother Thomas. You're in 610, Holy Mother.'

When it stopped, they rushed out of the elevator and looked at the signs telling them where to find their rooms. 'I'll abandon you here if you don't mind,' said Mrs Bronson, 'and we'll meet again at breakfast. Sleep well. It must have been awful ...' She descended.

'This way, brothers,' said the abbot.

Led by Jerry Cornelius and Karen von Krupp the monks trudged off down the corridor. They turned right, turned left and found the rooms. All the doors were painted turquoise with yellow numbers.

Jerry stopped outside his door.

Karen stopped outside her door.

The monks put their keys into their locks and opened their doors and went inside, closing the doors.

'See you later,' said Jerry.

She shrugged.

Jerry entered his room and turned on the light.

It was a small, narrow room with a couch that converted to a bed, a single window at the far end with turquoise drapes. He switched on the set and got the time, the temperature and the humidity. He adjusted his watches, pulled off his cassock and checked his blue silk suit for wrinkles. It had survived pretty well.

The bathroom was near the door. It had a shower, a sink and a lavatory. The towels were turquoise edged with gold. The shower curtains were yellow. The soap was turquoise. The tiles were green and orange. Jerry turned on the shower.

He went back into the room and took off his clothes, carrying his holstered vibragun with him to the bathroom and hanging it on the towel rail. He stepped under the boiling shower, soaping himself all over and humming Jimi Hendrix's *May This be Love* to himself.

As he dried, Jerry called room service and ordered the quart of Jack Daniel's Black Label, the Onion Soup au Gratin Mouquin, the Sautéed Calf's Liver with Smothered Onion, Hickory Smoked Bacon and Home Fried Potatoes, the piece of Old New York Cheese Cake, the Two Flavour Jello with whipped cream and the Pot of Steaming Freshly Brewed Coffee. He gave his room number and his name as Father Jeremiah Cornelius.

He called the main desk.

'This is Father Cornelius. Has Bishop Beesley checked in, do you know?'

'I'm sorry, sir. No Bishop Beesley.'

'Thank you. God bless you.'

Room service arrived. There was something to be said for civilization, really. Jerry set to eating.

When he had finished the food, he poured himself a large glass of bourbon and drank it down.

One thing was certain; America was the last decent country to eat in.

Now he was ready for almost anything.

He unwrapped the towel from his waist and pulled the

cassock over his head.

The sign on his door warned him to lock it carefully in case of prowlers. He ignored the sign and crossed to Karen's door.

He turned the handle. The door wasn't locked. He opened it a crack. The light was on. He slipped inside.

At first all he noticed were Karen's legs tightly wrapped around the heaving buttocks of Brother Thomas. She looked over the monk's white shoulder and raised her eyebrows.

'You can go off people, you know,' she said.

'Oh, fuck,' said Jerry miserably.

2. He Won't Have to Beg Me – Tonight

Jerry pulled up the blind, yearning for music, and stared out at the American morning.

It wasn't all beer and skittles. Even the educational channel was playing Gilbert and Sullivan. He had been sick twice in the night and had finally turned the television off.

Abandoning the cassock, he clad himself in yellow silk with a wide red tie knotted under the flowing collar of his white shirt. His soft calf boots, by Raviana, enclosed his feet and the vibragun cheered him up a little. Perhaps it was time to kill someone.

He combed his milk-white hair in front of the mirror, sweeping it down and then up to form two wings framing his graceful black face.

'Astatic,' he murmured cheerfully before his thoughts returned to Karen.

As he entered the corridor, he glanced across at her door, hesitated and then continued towards the elevators.

He wasn't often in love, after all. Not that sort of love. Could it be that that was giving him the identity trouble? It was worse than he'd expected. There had been a certain difficulty in focussing ever since he and Karen had left London. A certain mistiness, a feeling of fragmentation.

He patted his vibragun under his jacket as he reached the elevator. It was his only link with reality, with the machine in the cellars at Ladbroke Grove.

Koutrouboussis...

The name came and went.

Memories of Soho faded.

He put his hand into the inside pocket of his jacket and pulled out a postcard. On it was a slightly blurred picture of a Tompion clock in an engraved steel case. On the other side was an address, JERRY CORNELIUS, AMERICA, and a message: HANG ON.

He thought of Baptist Charbonneau and Kit Carson, of

Humphrey Bogart and Kirk Douglas, of George Washington and Franklin D. Roosevelt, of Herman Melville and Dashiell Hammett, and he thought particularly of Charles Ives, Lead-belly, Woody Guthrie and Jimi Hendrix.

Tears came to his eyes and he leaned heavily against the wall until the elevator arrived. America, the shattered dream, the broken promise ...

At breakfast he couldn't eat his scrambled eggs, and his English Muffin also went untasted. He drank a lot of coffee and for an hour read Jack Trevor Story's *Hitler Needs You* which cheered him up, as he had known it would.

The monks and nuns were all seated at another table, staring at him incredulously. Karen was nowhere in sight, but Jerry saw a face he recognized.

It was Protz. A Russian agent and almost certainly a double agent for the Israelis. Could the archaically dressed man be interested in him?

Protz tripped from the crowded restaurant almost as soon as Jerry had spotted him. Remembering his encounter with Pyat the Chekist, Jerry began to feel nervous.

Mr Silver appeared behind him. 'Father Abbot? The arrangements ...'

It wasn't like Jerry to lie. It surprised him as he said shiftily, 'Not "abbot" if you don't mind, my dear Mr Silver – Chuzzle-wit – I'm afraid there are enemies who have succeeded in following me to this – even this – sanctuary ...'

'The police?'

'What could they prove? No, no. I thank you for your concern, but do not worry. I have friends, you see, in New York. They'll pick me up later. Bishop Beesley ...'

'Oh, Bishop Beesley! Good hands. God bless you.' Mr Silver backed secretively away.

'God bless *you*, Mr Silver ...'

'No, God ... Nice of you, Father – Chuzzlewit – thanks again ...' Mr Silver dropped his eyes. 'God ... thank you, Mr ...'

Jerry whirled on his heel and went softly away from the restaurant, bought some Shermans in the lobby and returned to his room.

*

He turned on the television and changed channels until he got the hotel's own closed circuit channel. It showed a broad view of the road outside the main exit. The road led across the plain to Manhattan. There was surprisingly little traffic. The channel was vision only and the room itself was sound-proofed. A sense of isolation overwhelmed him.

He went to the window and saw a Pan Am 727 shimmer into the sky.

If Protz were in the States, then Pyat could be here, too. Pyat would tip off Beesley. Beesley would come to the hotel.

Why was he waiting for Beesley to come to him? Impulsively he went to the mirror. His skin had turned a deep brown, his eyes were uncomfortable.

If he hired a car he could be in New York in half an hour. He would be all right in New York. But Karen wouldn't come with him.

In the distance, the sun beat on the towers of the shining city.

There was no escape.

He took off his jacket, switched channels, watched five minutes of *The Good, the Bad and the Ugly* before the quality of the colour upset him, poured himself a glass of Jack Daniel's, sipped it, put his jacket back on, went out of his room and opened Karen's door.

She had gone. Her suitcase was gone.

Jerry took his lighter from his pocket and tried to set fire to the messy bed. But the sheets were too sweaty. They wouldn't burn.

3. A Psychologist Reveals the Sexual Overtones of the Monster Movies

For three days Jerry stared at the television and the view of the street. On the highway there were increasing numbers of motorcycle cops in unfamiliar black uniforms and helmets. Frequently, during the day or night they would arrest a driver for no evident offence.

Once he switched to a news programme. Someone referred to the European disease that was sweeping the country. 'The only answer to it is the European cure . . .'

His meals were now brought to his room, but he had lost his taste for hotel living. When he had last appeared in the restaurant it was to see Karen with Protz. She had looked bored. On her way out he tried to trip her up but failed.

He had watched her bottom for a sign, but got nothing.

The lack of music was beginning to disturb him much more than Karen. A flutter of brushes on a skin, a whine or two from a Martin, a thud from a Fender bass; anything would have helped. But there wasn't a note in the entire hotel. Nothing, anyway, that wasn't offensive quasi-music, such as the Gilbert and Sullivan.

His vague feelings of discomfort had grown by the fourth day. The police arrests seemed increasingly arbitrary.

He turned on the television to a news broadcast for the second time.

President Paolozzi had disappeared and had been replaced by his Vice President, Konnie Agonosto, who was promising to restore order as quickly as possible.

A little while later President Ronald Boyle, elected by emergency vote, announced that his special militia were already getting the country back on a safe, sane, orderly footing, ready to honour her commitments anywhere at home or in the world.

Jerry packed his case and put it near the door. He hurried into Karen's empty room and picked up the phone. 'Can you give me Mr Protz's room number?'

Protz was in 805. Jerry went up by the service stairs, found 805 and knocked on the door.

'*Was is das?*'

'Karen. It's Jerry. We're in trouble I think. You'd better pack.'

'Please go away, Jerry. I'm not going to be tricked ...'

'Okay.'

He walked down the corridor. Everywhere there were open doors and he could see people hastily pushing their possessions into their luggage. He went back to 805, kicking fiercely at the door.

'Karen. Everyone's getting out.'

'Go away. Why?'

'Something's up. A change of government.' Down the hall came a few bars of Chuck Berry which were rapidly cut off.

Jerry began to pant. Karen knew what she was doing. Koutrouboussis ... How elaborate was the plot? There had never been so much pressure before. He was out of his element. Everything was threatened.

George Catlin – Mark Twain – Henry Ford. It was no good. The postcard in his pocket was thin and wrinkled. As he touched it, it crumbled.

The door opened. Pyat stood there. His eyes were sardonic. 'What sort of thing, Comrade Cornelius, is up?'

'The poor sods,' said Jerry. 'The poor bloody sods. Is this your doing? You traitor ...'

'Think of Frank, Comrade Cornelius. Your brother. What would he have done?'

'Uncle Frank...' Jerry's brain misted over again. 'Where's ... ?'

'You look out of sorts, comrade.'

'You were the one, weren't you? You set the trap?'

'Nonsense. I'm merely an advisor over here.'

'Tell Doktor von Krupp I'll wait in my room for her.'

Jerry walked as steadily as he could to the stairs and began to climb down them. His teeth were aching.

4. The Beauty the Reds Can't Forget

On the TV Jerry watched the people hurry from the hotel and be scooped up by formations of Boyle's militia. It was rather like watching a ballet.

Three black Cadillacs, their windows gleaming dark one-way glass, came down the road towards the hotel. Things looked sticky for the visitors.

'Jerry.'

He turned.

Karen had her case with her. Jerry picked up his own. 'Got your passport? We're going back.'

'So soon?'

'I know it's disappointing...'

The corridors were empty. They took the elevator to the main lobby where a few people, with anxious, bewildered faces, stood about.

A small man in a brown leather trench coat bent his swarthy, severe face over people's passports. It was Mr Silver or someone very much like him. He was obviously in charge now.

Jerry strolled to the desk. 'I'll pay if I may.'

'Of course, sir. 604 and 610, is that right?' The brunette leafed through a desk file.

'That's right.'

'There you are, sir.' She handed him the bills. 'Two hundred and fifty dollars, please.'

'I can give you American Express traveller's cheques.'

'I'm sorry, sir.'

'Carte Blanche...?'

'Cash only, sir. It's the new rule.'

Jerry slipped his hand into his back pocket and saw that the man in the trench coat was approaching Karen, a triumphant look in his eyes.

Jerry gave the girl his last three hundred dollar bills.

'Keep the change.'

'I can't do that, sir.' She gave a prim gasp.

'It's all shifting backwards, pilgrim.' Jerry got to Karen before the man who looked like Mr Silver. If it was Mr Silver he pretended he didn't remember Jerry.

'Let me see your passports.'

'We're foreign nationals ...' Jerry realized that this was no longer protection. They were on their own. But then, hadn't he always been on his own? He frowned.

'You don't look well,' said Mr Silver. 'Anything worrying you?'

'How should I know?'

'What are you calling yourself?' A look of disdain crossed Mr Silver's face.

'Jeremiah Cornelius. Jeremiah Cornelius.'

'Okay. You're suspected of aiding agents of forces hostile to the United States government. We'll have to search your luggage.'

'Go ahead.' Then Jerry noted the expression on Karen's face.

Silver signalled to two tall men in plastileather trench coats. 'Taylor. Dunlop.' They picked up the expensive bags.

'The keys?' Mr Silver held out his damp hand.

'They're unlocked.'

Taylor opened Jerry's case first and pawed disgustedly through the coloured silks. When he looked back up Jerry knew he didn't have a chance.

'What about her?' Jerry indicated Karen. 'Let her on the plane, won't you? She's just a girl who came along. A secretary ...'

'You employ her, do you?' Dunlop laughed.

'She's not your wife, is she?' Mr Silver curled his lip. 'You aliens! Check her case.'

Jerry hung loose. He lit a Romeo y Julieta.

'That's a nice cigar,' said Silver sniffing. He nodded as his men brought something out of Karen's bag. 'You've got it. I like the smell of a good cigar.' It was a small gold model of an Apollo rocket. 'Okay. Now let's see those passports.'

Karen glanced at Jerry as she gave her passport to Silver. Had she been conned by Protz and Pyat? How elaborate was the set-up? Silver knew there were ambiguities but wasn't admitting it. He was going after them merely because he didn't like them. That was how things were.

'German,' said Silver. 'And British, eh? Where you from, bwah?'

'Britain.'

'Before that?'

'Heaven?'

'That in the West Indies?'

'My father didn't say.'

'I'll keep the passports. They look like crude forgeries to me. Your picture's in negative, even.'

'Check it.'

'We will. Taylor. Dunlop. Get them on the bus with the rest.'

The two tall men took Jerry and Karen by the arm and guided them through the lobby, then through the swing doors to where a big airport bus waited. There were a lot of people already inside.

As they came out on the sidewalk Jerry saw people run and cars swerve as a Boeing 707 swung off the runway and, jets screaming, taxied between the airport buildings to cross the highway at an angle and slither across a field.

'You boys certainly have everything working for you.' Jerry threw his cigar in the gutter.

'On the bus,' said Taylor.

Jerry and Karen climbed aboard. The bus was decorated in chrome and light blue. All the seats were full of nervous people, mostly middle-aged and middle-class. That was something, thought Jerry.

One well set up man in a grey topcoat and hat held an expensive briefcase against his chest. He wore brown leather gloves. 'I'm Feldman,' he said. 'Feldman. I'm Feldman.'

'That's it,' Dunlop told the driver. 'You can close the doors.'

Feldman dashed forward as the doors began to shut. Taylor hit him in the face. Feldman staggered back, his nose bleeding.

The bus moved out with Jerry and Karen clinging to the slippery central pole. From the hotel came the sound of Thompson sub-machine guns.

The bus reached an intersection and turned inland, away from New York.

Soon they were on Interstate 80.

Jerry felt a tugging at his jacket and he looked down into the heavily made-up face of an old woman with a blue rinse who sat in the nearest seat. 'Young man,' she whispered, 'is this the Ithaca bus?'

'You'd better ask the driver, ma'am,' Jerry told her. 'I'm not sure we're going that far.'

The Lance battlefield missile can go anywhere the Army needs to go.

It's rugged, it's accurate. It's easy to operate.

And . . . it's mobile.

It can be moved into action by helicopter, air-dropped by parachute or carried by ground vehicles over rough terrain under all weather conditions.

The Lance light-weight launcher can be towed by some of the smallest vehicles in the inventory, down to the $\frac{1}{4}$-ton size. The basic launcher frame and missile frame and missile fit into a full-tracked carrier for land or water surface mobility.

And, it only takes a six-man crew to operate each Lance system.

It is propelled by a storable, pre-packaged liquid propulsion system – the first Army missile so powered.

Lance is almost as portable as its ancient namesake, the basic weapon of the warrior since time began.

'Lance mobility,' LTV ad

1. Mail Order Bride from Pennsylvania

Somewhere in Pennsylvania, in thickly wooded hills overlooking the Delaware, the bus stopped by a tall barbed wire fence bearing a wooden notice board that said KEEP OUT – GOVT. PROTECTED EXPERIMENTAL NATURE RESERVE.

'Okay, everybody.' The driver took a Swiss M11 Carbine from under his seat. 'Here's where you spend your vacation.'

Taylor and Dunlop glanced at him disapprovingly. The blue doors hissed open and the passengers piled out into the narrow dirt road that ran beside the wire.

Jerry's spirits were rising. As he left the bus, he tipped the driver a dollar.

'This way,' said Dunlop.

Struggling with their heavy suitcases, the passengers followed Taylor and Dunlop until they reached a decorative wrought-iron gate in front of a small Bavarian-style lodge from which three armed militia men, in the black uniforms, the mirror sunglasses and the motorcycle helmets, emerged.

A fourth militia man poked his head out of the whimsically carved doorway. 'Wait there. I'll call the camp.'

Jerry gripped two curling bits of black metal and peered through the gate, breathing in the gentle scent of pines. A wide track led between the trees on the other side of the wire and disappeared over a rise. Beyond the rise a diesel engine whined and a big Ford articulated freight truck came bumping into sight and, sounding the twin golden horns on its roof, swung round in the clearing near the ledge. The driver jumped down from his cab and ran to open the sliding doors of the truck.

One of the militia men unlocked the wrought-iron gate. 'Okay. Come on through.'

The passengers trudged up to the freight wagon and got awkwardly aboard.

Jerry helped the old lady clamber in.

'It stinks of meat.' She leaned on his shoulder. 'Of animals.

What the hell is the company doing to us?'

'It's only a short ride, ma'am.' Jerry assisted Karen, relishing the texture of the rough tweed on his palm. 'We'll soon be there.'

As the doors of the car slid shut and the engine started up, Jerry crouched in a corner in the semi-darkness and they bumped through the woods. Five minutes later the truck braked and the outside air rang with cheerful shouts until it moved on a few yards, stopped again, and cut off its engine.

They blinked as the doors slid open to reveal a surly sergeant who waved them out with his rifle.

Mr Feldman had recovered slightly. He stood in the yard dusting himself down as his fellow passengers disembarked and looked incuriously round at the long wooden huts and the triple fence of barbed wire that had armed observation towers every thirty feet. 'Who's in charge here?' demanded Mr Feldman. 'I have some questions to ask.'

'You want the Camp Governor,' the surly sergeant told him. 'He'll be talking to you in a few minutes.'

Jerry began to whistle. Karen looked at him with a mixture of contempt, suspicion and panic.

There was a chance of a break, after all.

2. How Soon Legal Polygamy?

The new arrivals stood in a long line facing the main hut and there was only the sound of the pine cones cracking in the heat until the door marked CAMP GOVERNOR creaked open and a tall, elegant man came out and saluted them.

The Camp Governor wore a uniform cut from fine, black needlecord and his cap was at just the right angle above his mirror sunglasses which were as black and as bright as his highly polished jackboots.

'Good afternoon, ladies and gentlemen. I am Captain Brunner, your governor. It is my duty and pleasure to ensure that you are properly looked after during your stay here. As you are no doubt aware, under the present emergency conditions laid down by our president, Mr Boyle, an in-depth and far-thinking piece of social experimentation is taking place and you are privileged to be part of the experiment which touches, to a degree, on the problems of over-population in this nation. You will, of course, be well treated and all your basic needs will be catered to. Western ...' He reached languidly for the clipboard which the sergeant handed him. 'We can assure you, however, that your internment will be as short as possible. We aim for a quick release.' He turned his attention to the clipboard. 'Now, could all professional men and wives of professional men over forty please raise their hands?'

Only Jerry and Karen von Krupp did not raise their hands.

'Excellent,' said Captain Brunner. 'You are all – or almost –' he glanced disapprovingly at Jerry and Karen – 'entitled to priority service. Are there any questions I can answer for you?'

Mr Feldman raised his hand. 'My name is Feldman. Can I call my wife and tell her where I am?'

'Even better, Mr Feldman – we are tracing your wife and she should be joining you soon. Yes, ma'am.'

'My name's Mrs Meriel McCarthy.'

'Yes?'

'I want to know what I am doing here.'

'Your maiden name?'

'Sullivan.'

'I see. Well, it's hard to explain in a word, Mrs McCarthy It's all part of President Boyle's Law and Order Campaign You believe in Law and Order, I hope?'

'Of course.'

'Then I'm sure you will be prepared to suffer a little inconvenience for a short time so that the president can make sure there's plenty of Law and Order in the future?'

'I guess so.'

'Fine. Well, I suppose you're all tired and dusty after your journey and want to wash-up. Leave your bags here and they will be taken to your accommodation. The sergeant will show you to the ablutions hut.'

The new arrivals followed the sergeant towards the hut with the tall chimney. Jerry and Karen were left standing among the abandoned suitcases.

'I'll deal with you two in my office.' Captain Brunner hung the clipboard on a hook by the door. 'Step inside, please.' He sauntered through the door which swung shut behind him.

Karen looked towards the disappearing line of people and then at Jerry. 'You seem in better shape,' she said.

'Not part of the plan, eh?' Jerry pushed open Captain Brunner's door. 'Come on in.'

Hesitantly, Karen followed him in. The office was beautifully furnished, with leather panelling and matching furniture. The view through the window showed a school yard in which happy children in little white smocks were playing.

Captain Brunner sat at his desk lighting a cigarette in a long, ivory holder. He had a sensitive face and long-fingered almost delicate, hands. He removed his sunglasses and regarded Jerry through sardonic crimson eyes.

'Well, well, well ... And what brings you to Camp Resurrection?'

'A series of circumstances, Captain Brunner. This is Dokto von Krupp.'

'Your mistress?'

'My ex-mistress.'

'How could that be possible? It seems, at this moment, M

110

Cornelius, to be a question of accretion more than anything else.'

'It does indeed.'

'We'll see what we can do about it. Soon. Why are you in the US? Looking for me, I hope.'

'I thought I was looking for a Bishop Beesley, but it's possible that I came to lose myself, as it were. Not anticipated, of course.'

'You can't run away from yourself, Mr Cornelius.'

'I hope you're right, captain. I feel better already.'

'So you should. You're in the shit, really, if you don't mind me telling you . . .'

'That was my impression.' Jerry tapped his skull. 'I was a bit out of sorts. When this Beesley pinched a batch of our best transmogs . . .'

'Still fishing, eh? Well, I know how it is. The last I heard of Beesley was at a party a week ago. He was in San Francisco, I gather, with his yacht.'

'With my patients?'

'Almost certainly. His main headquarters are nearby – in Los Angeles.'

'Is he working for your boss? This Boyle?'

'Good heavens, no. Beesley may be crude, but he's not that crude. He has nothing to do with the creation of Greater America. Is the name Nye familiar?'

'No.'

'Well, he's vaguely connected with that name in some way. A Faustian character, your Bishop Beesley, really.'

'I wouldn't say that,' said Karen von Krupp.

'Doubtless you know him better than I.' Captain Brunner removed his cap and placed it neatly on the desk. His short hair was as white as Jerry's He undid his tunic collar.

Karen von Krupp was frowning. 'Are you responsible for this situation, Captain Brunner?'

'Indirectly, yes. Now, Jerry, we'll have to think of getting you out of here, won't we?'

'I suppose so.'

'It's obvious you can't stay. You'll have to escape and perhaps you'd better kill me at the same time. I presume you've a needle-gun with you.'

'Vibragun.'

'So it's vibraguns now, is it? Well, well. That'll do, anyhow. It will be a relief.'

'To both of us.'

'Yes, indeed.'

'I was wondering if there was a Shift Tunnel handy.'

'In America? You must be joking. This is a stable country, Mr Cornelius. Even I can't produce miracles!'

Jerry laughed. 'A helicopter, then? Or a light plane?'

'The best I can offer is that diesel truck. Unless ...' he raised his hands in a helpless gesture. 'We're in the sticks, here, Mr Cornelius.'

'Okay. What shall we do now?'

'Wait in my office until I return. There are very few books, I'm afraid. Watch the children playing. Aren't they sweet? Do you love children as much as me?'

'Naturally.'

3. The Old Hollywood Spirit Never Dies

Captain Brunner soon came back. 'I'd forgotten I wouldn't be needing the Duesenberg. You can take that, if you like.'

Jerry nodded. 'Why had you forgotten?'

'It was returned just this morning. My chauffeur borrowed it and got caught on a carefree driving rap. He was shot yesterday. Even I couldn't get him off that one.'

They laughed together.

Karen von Krupp sucked at her teeth. There was a tiny spot of blood in the middle of her lower lip. She had tense hands.

'I don't know,' said Jerry, 'whether to go to Frisco and risk it or try to make for somewhere else, under the circumstances. You'd know best.'

'True enough. But I don't want to influence your decision, Mr Cornelius. See how it works out.'

'Certainly. Now, are we going to make this a spectacular?'

'Why not?'

'Okay. Don't look so defeated, Karen. You can't win them all. Are you coming with me?'

'I'm staying here.'

'Is that a good idea, do you think? Beesley ...'

'Failure is failure. I'm staying.'

'In what capacity?' Brunner asked politely.

She shrugged and her looks faded. 'I don't much care. It's peaceful here.'

Jerry gave her shoulder a sympathetic pat. 'You know, I should really shoot you. It's the policy.'

She continued to suck at her teeth.

'That adds a new wrinkle.' Jerry winked at her.

A tear fell out of her eye.

'Let her stay here,' Captain Brunner suggested. 'I'm sure she'll go far, when she gets over it.'

'But Beesley ...'

'Will it make a lot of difference?'

'Time's silting up.'

'You're right, I suppose.' Jerry grinned. 'Sweet dreams, Karen.'

'Off we go, then.' Captain Brunner danced for the door.

'Off we go.'

Off they went, with Jerry pushing Captain Brunner ahead of him with his vibragun and Captain Brunner calling in a delicious treble, 'Do as he orders! Do as he orders!'

The big Duesenberg – three tons, supercharged, built 1936 with its bullet-proof windows and steel shutters – was outside.

They climbed in.

Captain Brunner drove and Jerry Cornelius pointed the vibragun at his head.

Black-uniformed guards milled around in excitement, trying to think of something positive. Then the wind took a turn and thick, yellow smoke from the chimneys got into their eyes and throats and made them cough. As they opened the gates of Camp Resurrection, most of them just looked embarrassed.

Standing outside the governor's office, Karen von Krupp waved almost sadly to Jerry.

'Good old Karen,' said Jerry.

Captain Brunner settled himself comfortably at the wheel as they drove through the pines that filtered the last of the evening sunshine.

'I must admit I'd prefer Casablanca,' he said. 'But that's all in the past now, I'm afraid. Or present. It depends which way you look at it.' He took a swig from the bottle of Bell's Cream Whisky in the clip by the steering wheel. 'The last bottle. It's just as well, in the circumstances. You don't mind if I go part of the way with you, do you, my dear boy?'

'Heaven forbid!' said Jerry. 'Of course not.'

They reached the next fence and the lodge. Someone had phoned the guards, for they had their guns ready but couldn't think of a use for them.

'Put the plates up, could you, Captain Brunner?' Jerry smiled at the guards.

Captain Brunner touched a button. The steel shutter moaned upwards and they were in darkness. Captain Brunner switched on the light.

'Now,' said Jerry. 'If you wouldn't mind ...'

'Say the word.'

'Consider it said.'

'And the word . . .'

Jerry smiled. 'Captain Brunner – you're a card, after my own heart.'

The plate on Jerry's window opened up until there was a hole five inches in diameter in the very centre. Jerry poked his gun through and took aim. The guards shook to pieces. He turned the gun and the gates quivered and creaked and fell down. They roared through.

'Hey ho for the open road,' sang Captain Brunner, turning the car in the general direction of Buffalo. 'Where were you thinking of for the honeymoon?'

'Where else?'

With a spontaneous gesture of affection, Captain Brunner flung his arm around Jerry's shoulders, hugged him tight, and stepped hard on the accelerator.

1. How the Israeli War Solved a Rape Murder!

The house was a splendid example of Carpenters Gothic, covered in turrets and eccentric dormer windows, with pointed towers and jigsaw scrollwork and shadowed verandas made to resemble a monks' walk. A somewhat tasteless note was the more recent cobblestone chimney.

Inside, the hall was dark and filled with a huge umbrella stand; a hat rack and a mirror that seemed to reflect the darkness. From the parlour came the damp, musty smell of horse-hair and mahogany, of marble, artificial flowers and antimacassars. On the other side of the hall the living room was full of mission furniture in oak and leatherette. Leading off the living room was the dining room with its table and chairs of golden oak and its view from the window over the Falls.

The house was still occupied.

Outside the empty streets echoed the whimpering roar of the water. The hotels and motel cabins, the souvenir shops, the restaurants and movie houses blended with the trees, the shrubs and the weeds. Sometimes the wind would move a yellow newspaper or a rusty can.

On their way to the border Captain Brunner had steered nostalgically through streets blocked with twisted automobiles. 'Ah, fickle fashion.' Most of the buildings had been looted, stripped and burned.

At the dining table they ate the individual TV Steak Chateaubriand Dinners Captain Brunner had brought up from the cold room in the basement.

'And how did you leave Europe?' Captain Brunner unbuttoned his uniform jacket to show a yellow shirt of Sea Island Cotton.

'Much as I hope to find it.' Jerry pushed his dinner away and took another sip of his Californian Riesling. 'It's an uphill struggle.'

'Perhaps it always will be, Jerry.'

'One door opens. Another closes.'

'Isn't that for the best?'

Jerry raised a jet-black hand to a jet-black face and rubbed his right eye. Captain Brunner smiled.

'The illusion of power,' said Jerry. 'It sometimes seems too sweet for words.'

'Or actions, for that matter.'

'Sure.'

'You've got rid of the *déjà vu* now, have you?'

'Not altogether.'

'Well ...' Captain Brunner stacked the half-eaten trays. 'I'll put these in the kitchen. Do you want to take a walk this afternoon?'

'A last walk ...'

'If you wish.'

'It's really up to you, you know.' Jerry turned to look at the Falls.

'I'm getting a bit reluctant to go. That's the trouble.'

'I know what you mean. Do you want to do it yourself?'

Captain Brunner picked up the empty bottle. 'That wouldn't be according to the rules.'

'The rules are very strict.'

'Stricter than you could believe.'

'All right. Mind you, I could do with some bloody music.' Jerry stood up.

'The victrola's over there.'

Jerry went into the living room to look at the big phonograph with its oak-veneered cabinet. He opened the cupboard at the bottom and pulled out the cumbersome 78s. They rattled in his hands. He opened the lid, wound the handle and put a record on the turntable.

When Captain Brunner came back into the room George M. Cohan was singing *Yankee Doodle* and Jerry lay on the mission couch staring up at the beams in the ceiling.

'I believe there's some good Al Jolsons and the whole of *Green Pastures* in there.' Captain Brunner hesitated on the threshold. 'That's going back a bit.'

'Before my time,' said Jerry.

'And mine.'

They listened to George M. Cohan with intense, clinical concentration.

'What does it tell us?' Captain Brunner stroked Jerry's hair.

'It's not a code we could ever hope to understand.' Jerry shrugged sadly.

'No.'

Systematically they broke the records and stacked the pieces inside the cabinet.

2. Why Artists are Going Back to Realism

'What must be must be,' said Captain Brunner.

It was dawn and the sun shone through the lace curtains o the bedroom.

He turned his head on the pillow and looked tenderly a Jerry who had just opened his eyes.

'This morning,' said Jerry.

'It's overdue.'

'Okay.'

Captain Brunner rose and stretched his beautiful body ther kneeling on the mattress, reached up and straightened the GOI BLESS OUR HOME pokerwork on the wall.

'You're looking old,' said Jerry. 'Used up.'

'Wouldn't you?'

'I guess my time will come.'

'We all get redundant. It's the one snag, really. Still, I'r glad I served a purpose.'

'An important one. Only you ...' Jerry swung out of bed Purposefully he began to dress. 'I've got work to do.'

'I don't think I'll wear anything today.' Captain Brunne opened the door. 'I'll see you downstairs.'

Jerry strapped on his shoulder holster and checked his gur He went along the landing to the bathroom and splashed col water over his face. He dried himself and descended to th kitchen where Captain Brunner had already prepared coffee.

'I'll feel much happier in myself,' said Jerry.

'And so will I. It's kind of you to have borne with me.'

'I can guess what it's like.'

'Of course.'

They finished their coffee and left the house, walking slowl through the deserted streets towards the Falls.

At last they stood on a promontory overlooking the hug mass of descending water. Spray splashed them. Drops water brightened Captain Brunner's body. He took a dee breath.

Jerry's eyes filled with tears. 'Relationships are awkward.'

His voice was drowned, but Captain Brunner nodded.

Jerry slipped the gun from under his coat. The water crashed down. It foamed and was blue-green, shining in the sun.

Suddenly Captain Brunner turned, shouted, pointed, and leapt off the ground in a perfect dive. Jerry watched him fall. Then he looked back.

Bishop Beesley, dressed in the full robes of his calling, held to his shoulder a Remington 1100 with a shell-flame maple stock. The rifle was pointed at Jerry. 'I'll have your gun, Mr Cornelius.'

'This is an inconvenient moment, bishop.'

'I apologize.'

From the cream and yellow Lincoln convertible behind him emerged the blonde girl Jerry had first met in Nibelburg. She held an identical Remington 1100 on her thigh and wore a mustard Feraud gym-slip dress of Terylene/wool worsted crêpe, a matching hat with a chocolate band and a wide, floppy brim, narrow net Lurex stockings, chocolate-brown Marano boots buttoned to the knee with pearls and a small bag of brushed calf hanging by a gold chain over one crooked elbow. Her white kid gloves were by Pittards.

'I wonder where you've been,' said Jerry.

'Bond Street,' she said. 'I'll kill you if you don't hand him the gun now.'

Jerry offered the vibragun by its barrel. Bishop Beesley lowered his own rifle, pushed back his mitre, wiped his brow with his free hand and then came forward to take the gun. 'I'm obliged.'

Jerry glanced back at the leaping foam. The noise from the Falls now seemed barely audible. He frowned.

'You've certainly given us a chase, Mr Cornelius,' Bishop Beesley said. 'We've come a long way to find you, you know. We thought at first you must have changed your identity. Would my good lady be with you?'

'I'm afraid not.'

'I'm sorry your friend rushed off ...'

'It's all one, really.'

'Was it a close friend?'

'He's been a father and mother to me in his time.'

'I admire your philosophy. Well, come along. We've a fair journey ahead of us. Mitzi, if you'll drive I'll keep an eye on Mr Cornelius.'

Mitzi looked moodily at Jerry. Bishop Beesley handed her the vibragun and curled his fat finger around the trigger of his Remington. He poked at Jerry with it. 'The car, Mr Cornelius. You can sit next to the driver.'

Mitzi put her rifle under the seat and started the car. Jerry went round to the other side and got in. Mitzi was wearing Miss Cardin cologne and he breathed it in with some pleasure. After Beesley had heaved himself into the back of the car, she put it into reverse, then swung it round and headed west away from the house.

'You're going to take my word about Karen, then?' Jerry said.

'Why not?' Bishop Beesley unpeeled a Tootsie Roll. 'Besides, we checked the house.'

Mitzi drove with a sureness Jerry found relaxing. He leant back and watched the buildings disappear

'You're not going over the border, then?'

'Not by the bridge, Mr Cornelius. Not under the circumstances.'

'What are the circumstances?'

'Why – you're being sought by government officials. There is even a reward for your arrest as an escaped prisoner. You are in hot water!'

'I wouldn't be too sure of that,' said Jerry reminiscently.

Bishop Beesley's mouth was full, so he shrugged

Soon Jerry noticed the Welland Canal. It was choked with small private craft, most of which had apparently been scuttled. Others bore shell-holes. There were still people aboard some of the houseboats He scratched his head as they drove along beside the canal.

The Bishop chewed noisily. 'They had nothing to fear but fear itself,' he said between mouthfuls. 'Poor things.'

'That's something to be afraid of.' Jerry saw black smoke in the distance. He wound down his window to smell it, but it was too far away.

'Would you mind shutting the window?' Bishop Beesley

rustled a paper bag. 'I'm subject to chills.'

Jerry wound the window back up.

'We could have the air-conditioning, if you like.' Beesley tapped Mitzi on the shoulder. 'Put it on, would you, dear.'

She reached out with her gloved hand, exposing several inches of pink flesh, and depressed a button. There came a whispering sound from below the dashboard.

'That's better, isn't it?' Bishop Beesley adjusted his hold on the rifle. 'Much better.'

'Every time.' Jerry settled back and closed his eyes. It had been a tiring week.

Stitching

LISTEN TO THE SOUNDS OF CRISIS!

Tune in to today's news as it actually happens!
Hear what goes on during an emergency. Monitor communications channels of police and fire departments. State Highway Patrols, Civil Defense Agencies, Coast Guard, and emergency services.

'ACTION!!' NEW PORTABLE POLICE RECEIVER $129.95, Riot, armed robbery, homicide, major fire, high speed chase ... the sounds of action and crisis are going on all around you every minute of the day. Now you can tune in on the police and fire radio frequencies in your area and actually hear the same communications as the police dispatcher and the men in the patrol cars and fire trucks. You'll hear the news as it's being made.

Nova-Tech ad, *True Police Cases*

1. Ashamed – When He Saw the Marks on My Body

When Jerry woke up it was late afternoon and the car was still moving down the wide, deserted highway. He saw a sign. They were heading for London.

'Is that where we're going?' Jerry asked Mitzi. She didn't reply.

'Don't disturb the driver, Mr Cornelius. You should know better than that.' Bishop Beesley tapped Jerry on the shoulder with a Mars Bar. 'No. We shan't be stopping at London. We've got a long way to go yet.'

Jerry looked at Mitzi's perfect features. 'She's got a lot of stamina,' he said admiringly.

'Mr Cornelius . . .'

Jerry noticed that they were almost out of fuel.

London came in sight. Part of the city was burning and a strange wailing noise filled the air. The car began to slow.

'Pogrom,' said Bishop Beesley. 'It's so close to the border, you see. We'd better transfer. Over there, Mitzi.' He pointed to the roadside which was now lined with low buildings. Most of them were stores. The neon signs were dead.

A Plymouth Barracuda, two of its wheels on the sidewalk, its doors open, was what the bishop had his eye on. Mitzi stopped the Lincoln. 'Have a look at the fuel gauge,' Bishop Beesley said.

Mitzi got out turned the key and peered in at the Plymouth's dashboard. She nodded; then she glanced at her dress. It clashed with the bright red Plymouth. She shook her head.

'Try the next one, then.'

Mitzi opened the door of a white Dodge Polara. 'Full,' she said.

'Out you get, Mr Cornelius.'

Jerry opened the door and swung his legs from the car. He got up and stretched. It was almost dark. The flames lit the city and the wailing was louder.

'Civil disturbance is nothing to worry about.' Bishop Beesley pushed him forward with the tip of the Remington. 'But Europe's in real trouble. No thanks to you.'

There was the noise of pistol fire and the bishop ducked. 'Hurry along, please, Mr Cornelius. Mitzi, will you get our stuff?'

After Bishop Beesley had climbed into the back Jerry sat in the front seat. More shots came from somewhere on the roofs above them, possibly from the liquor store with the half-lit neon sign, L N N I S L N N L Q R BEST.

Mitzi got the Dodge's trunk open and crammed the gear in. Jerry saw her weigh his vibragun in her hand and then put it in her handbag.

She climbed hurriedly into the driving seat and her skirt rose up showing Lurex thighs. Jerry took a deep breath. She tossed a white paper bag to the bishop.

Mitzi turned the key in the ignition. Jerry placed the tips of the fingers of his right hand on his knee and trembled. The car started. Mitzi spun the wheel. Jerry felt a tightness about his ribs and undid the buttons of his jacket.

Soon they had left the wailing city behind and the headlights glared on the wide, white road. Jerry clenched his hands together. 'You share the same faith, I take it?' He winked at Mitzi.

'More than that, Mr Cornelius.' Bishop Beesley's voice was slurred.

'There were a lot of planes,' Mitzi said quietly. 'But they seem to have disappeared.'

'They were going somewhere, my dear.'

'And tanks and so on . . .'

'Those, too.' Beesley laughed. 'You'd think there was an invasion or something!'

'A general mobilization?' Jerry lit a Punch Manuel Lopez, his last.

'You could say that. We must hand it to the Americans. When they set out to do a thing, they don't waste any time. President Boyle and his Greater American Party will soon have the planes landing on schedule.'

'Don't you feel something of a hypocrite?' Jerry glanced back at the bishop. 'I mean, you should hand me over to the authorities, by rights. I can't help feeling a bit guilty.'

'Things will take a while to settle down, Mr Cornelius. I am doing what is best for everyone. America will soon be on her feet again. And she will be cleaner.'

'I thought they were doing okay before.'

'You would. Not that I don't understand your views, of course. I do not mean to criticize. I believe in everybody having a say. Free will, Mr Cornelius. That's what the good God gave us, heaven help us.'

'Amen.'

'But there is a difference between free will, I would point out, and insane nihilism.'

'Naturally.'

'And anarchy. We are put on this earth to order it. The rhythm of the spheres, you know.'

'I could do with any bloody sort of rhythm right now.'

'Wait till we get to San Francisco.'

'*Buenas noches.*' Jerry fell asleep again.

'Everywhere seems red tonight,' Mitzi spoke with faint disapproval and woke Jerry up as she put the handbrake on.

'Where are we?' Jerry sat up.

'Port Huron. If you wouldn't mind, Mr Cornelius, I should like to leave the car.' Bishop Beesley moved and there was a crackle of paper wrappings. The back seat was a mass of litter.

Jerry opened the door and got slowly from the car, pulling back the seat to allow Bishop Beesley to heave himself out.

The car was parked on a wharf. Tied up at the wharf was an elegant steam yacht of about 700 tons and about 180 feet long. Jerry made out the name.

'*Teddy Bear,*' he said. 'That's a nice name.'

There were no lights on the wharf. Water lapped against the ship.

'Shall we go aboard, Mr Cornelius? Mitzi?'

Mitzi took the bags from the trunk and carried them towards the gangway. Jerry followed her. Bishop Beesley came last.

On deck Mitzi put down the bags and went forward to the bridge. From the shadows a tall, emaciated sailor appeared. He was dressed in a yellow uniform with a yellow cap and a flat, sallow face. He made a hasty salute that was half a bow. 'Evening, captain,' he whispered.

'Evening, steward. I believe you know Mr Cornelius.'

'Please to meet you, sir.' The steward looked shiftily at Jerry.

'You're one of ours, aren't you?' Jerry glanced chidingly at Beesley. 'The ex-chairman of the Arts Council, as I live and breathe. Jesus, Beesley, is this the best you can do?'

'He's not queer any more, at any rate!'

The steward gave a guilty grunt.

'He's not rich, either.' Jerry rubbed his nose. 'At least he was rich.'

'The meek, Mr Cornelius ...'

'You're a bit inept in my opinion, Bishop Beesley.'

'We've had to use inferior equipment, thanks to you.'

'You're not kidding.'

'Well, don't blame me, Mr Cornelius. Who started it, after all? It's you people who meddle. Transmogrification. It's a farce!'

'Excuse me, sir,' whispered the ex-chairman of the Arts

Council, 'but shall we slip out of port now, as you instructed?'

'Quietly, steward. Yes, yes.'

'People are happier,' said Jerry.

'Happiness? What's that? Happiness should come from a sense of self-fulfilment!'

'I'd have thought so.'

'Are you happy? In your anarchy?'

'Am I complaining?'

'Well, we're going to help you.'

'Not drag again?'

'That wasn't my idea. I agree it was crude. It was an emergency. A cruise is what you need.'

'Where's my cabin?'

'The steward knows.'

'Aren't you going to tell me?'

'Why should I?'

'Lead on, steward.'

'You're not in Europe now, Mr Cornelius. We're in control here, you know!'

'I'm famished.' Jerry followed the ex-chairman of the Arts Council along the deck.

'You'll get something to eat in a moment,' Beesley called. He had gone red.

'Not that kind of famished.' Jerry felt sleepy again. It was his only comfort. 'I need something more mutual than a meal.'

2. I'll Make Him Pay for What He Did to Me

They were on Lake Superior by the time Jerry, somewhat revitalized, but by no means himself, went up on deck and breathed in the stink.

'Why don't you stop fighting us, Herr Cornelius?' Mitzi leaned on the rail and stared out at the distant Michigan shore. The yacht was making good speed through the slime.

Mitzi wore an embroidered night-sky-blue cotton waistcoat tied with tiny black threads, dark and light blue flower-printed harem hipster trousers, sea-blue necklace, braided necklace with yellow tassels, blue Giselle silk scarves bound into a bandanna around her head, golden diamanté belt, turquoise and gold pin and armlets by Cadoro, with silver block-heeled sandals on her lovely little feet.

Her only make-up was her lipstick: Guerlain's Gremoble if Jerry wasn't mistaken. She smiled. 'Cheer up.' She handed him a set of filters for his nose.

'You look like a dream of Jamaica. Did I say I felt cheerless?'

'Well, you are our prisoner. What did happen to Karen von Krupp, by the way?'

'To the best of my knowledge she went into the catering trade. In Pennsylvania somewhere. It was all a bit complicated. We both had problems.'

'I can understand that. I expect she's too embarrassed to look us up.' Mitzi turned her face towards the pale blue sky and sniffed the wind. 'I don't bear her any grudge. Who could?'

'Who?'

'The planes have stopped.'

'You noticed that two nights ago.'

'Did I? Which planes? Do you have a personality problem, Herr Cornelius?'

'From time to time.'

'You would say that.' She laughed.

'I wish there was some bloody sustenance around here.'

Jerry looked over the rail at the foaming algae. 'It's hard going, Mitzi, I don't mind telling you.'

'What's your favourite food? Liver?'

'Not since they killed all the buffalo. It's not for me to say.'

'Are you really Jerry Cornelius?'

'Ah.' Jerry took a pace along the rail and gave her a wary wink.

'Aren't you an impostor?'

'Oho.'

'We're going through the new St Croix Canal, you know.'

'And then?'

'Along the Mississippi down to New Orleans.'

'You're very forthcoming.'

'Into the Gulf of Mexico. Through the Panama Canal and into the Pacific until we berth in San Francisco.'

'I get it.'

'Why don't you stop fighting us, Herr Cornelius? You know in your heart that we're right.'

'When does the next jolly boat leave?'

'The *Teddy Bear* has no jolly boats.'

'I am in a pickle, aren't I?'

'How do you feel?'

'Sleepy.'

'The long voyage will do you good.'

'I wish I could have stopped off in New York.'

'New York's rather hectic.'

'I have quite a lot of urgent business, you know.'

'It won't seem so urgent by the time we get to San Francisco.'

Jerry shook his head. 'I could do with a change of scenery.'

'You won't get it. You'll grow to like this scenery.'

'Christ!'

'Really, Mr Cornelius!' Bishop Beesley came waddling down the deck.

'What the fuck do you know about it?'

'That's a nice thing to say!'

Jerry looked at the algae again.

'It's a long way, Mr Cornelius.'

'Yeah.'

'I don't think you'd make it.'

'No.'

Mitzi folded her arms. 'You're not much of a catch.'

'I'm not the catch I'm worrying about. My patients ...'

'I've almost lost mine, Mr Cornelius.' Bishop Beesley smacked his lips over a Walnut Whip.

'I wish that was true. I'm going back to bed.'

'You'll have to wake up sooner or later.'

'Says who?' Jerry went down the companionway, opened the door of his neat, white cabin and fell on his bunk.

He was in a spot.

He'd have to try and bide his time. St Paul was his only hope.

3. My Sleep-Talking Shocked My Husband

Abbott; Abbey; Abell; Abercrombie; Abernethy; Ablett; Abraham; Abram; Absalom; Acheson; Acker; Acklam; Acres; Acton; Adair; Adam; Adcock; Adkins; Adlam; Adlard; Adlum; Adney; Adrain; Aga; Agate; Aiken; Alan; Alban; Albert; Alden; Alexander; Alfred; Alison; Allard; Allibon; Alsop; Ambler; Ambrose; Amos; Ampleford; Anderson; Angel; Anstey; Applegarth; Arkle; Armistead; Armstrong; Arrowsmith; Ashe; Aspinal; Attwood; Auger; Austin; Aylmer; Aysh; Babbitt; Bailey; Bairnsfeather; Baker; Bancroft; Bank; Barbary; Barclay; Bardell; Barker; Barlowe, Barnes; Barnett; Bartholomew; Barton; Barwick; Bateman; Batt; Baxter; Beach; Beauchamp; Beavis; Beckett; Bedwell; Belcher; Bell; Bellhanger; Bennett; Berrington; Beverley; Beynon; Biddulph; Bigg; Bingley; Birtwhistle; Bishop; Blackadder; Blackmore; Blackshaw; Blackwell; Blackwood; Blagrave; Blake; Blanchard; Blanchflower; Blandamore; Blenkinsop; Blennerhassett; Blight; Blood; Bloomer; Blunt; Blythe; Boatswain; Bolinbroke; Bond; Booth; Bouverie; Bowen; Bowie; Brabazon; Bradbourne; Bradbury; Brand; Brannan; Breakspear; Brereton; Brewer; Bridger; Brigham; Bristowe; Broadbent; Brockless; Brown; Bruce; Buchan; Buckmaster; Budd; Burgess; Burnes; Burstall; Burton; Bury; Butler; Buxton; Byford; Byron; Bywood; Caborne; Caesar; Caffin; Caldecott; Calder; Caldwell; Calver; Cambridge; Campbell; Cannan; Capstack; Carter; Cary; Caswell; Catchpole; Catmur; Catton; Chamberlain; Chandler; Charlton; Charteris; Chatterley; Cheetham; Chenevix; Childe; Chivers; Cholmondeley; Christey; Christian; Christin; Christmas; Christopher; Chrystal; Church; Churchill; Clachar; Clapham; Clarewood; Clarke; Clayton; Cleave; Clement: Clifford; Cock; Coffin; Cole; Coleman; Coleridge; Combe; Constantine; Cooke; Copperthwaite; Cordiner; Corfe; Corley; Cornelius . . .

Aaron; Abel; Abigail; Abraham; Absalom; Ada; Adalbert; Adam; Adela; Adelaide; Adeline; Adolphus; Adrian; Aeneas;

Afra; Agatha; Agnes; Alexis; Alice; Almeric; Aloys; Alphonsus; Amyas; Andrew; Angus; Ann; Anthony; Archibald; Arthur; Audrey; Augustus; Aylmer; Baldwin; Basil; Belle; Benedict; Bernard; Brian; Camilla; Candida; Caspar; Catherine; Chloe; Christabel; Christopher; Clara; Clovis; Constance; Cosmo; Cyriac; Cyrus; Daisy; Daphne; David; Deirdre; Dennis; Dinah; Dolores; Dominic; Doreen; Dorothy; Douglas; Duncan; Ebenezer; Edgar; Edwin; Eileen; Elias; Elizabeth; Elric; Emily; Emmanuel; Ena; Enoch; Eric; Ermentrude; Eustace; Ezra; Fabian; Faith; Fanny; Felix; Fergus; Freda; Fulke; Gabriel; Gareth; Gavin; George; Gertrude; Gervase; Gladys; Grizel; Gustavus; Gwyneth; Hadrian; Hamish; Harriet; Heloise; Henry; Herbert; Hercules; Hester; Hezekiah; Hilary; Hope; Hubert; Humphrey; Hyacinth; Ian; Ida; Igor; Ingeborg; Ingram; Isabella; Isaiah; Israel; Ivan; Ivy; Jabez; Jack; Jacob; James; Jane; Jasper; Jean; Jedidiah; Jenny; Jeremiah ...

JEREMIAH (Yah is high, or heals, or founds)
CORNELIUS (probably related to L. *cornu*, horn. –
        Dims. Corney, Corny. – Fem. Cornelia)

JEREMIAH CORNELIUS.
  His mouth was dry and his eyes were dim.
  Environment trouble.
  Identity trouble.
  Registration number : 1
  Father : Dead or whereabouts unknown.
  Mother : Living in Notting Hill.
  Relatives : Dead or whereabouts unknown.
  Residence : No fixed address.
  Physical characteristics : Mutable.
  Associates : Variable.
  Psychological situation : Weak.
  Position : Threatened.
  Emotional situation : Desperate.
  Recommendations : Hang on.
JEREMIAH CORNELIUS.
  The ship rolled.

*

JEREMIAH CORNELIUS.
  He was sick.
JEREMIAH CORNELIUS.
  Inside and out.
JEREMIAH CORNELIUS.
  Hang on.
JEREMIAH CORNELIUS.
  Get out.

4. The Rape-Goon Who Took a Nap with a Corpse!

Jerry opened up his eyes. He had lost all track of time, but there was daylight coming through the porthole. Lying alongside him was Mitzi's soft, warm body. She was pressing his hand to her privates.

'Do you mind?' said Jerry.

'Not if you don't.'

He pulled himself together. He still had some strength left, but it couldn't last much longer.

He saw her clothes were strewn across the cabin floor and there was her little handbag.

'Where are we?' he murmured, stroking her parted lips with his dark finger.

'Minneapolis is in sight.'

'In a pig's eye!'

'Oh! I saw it!'

'Okay. What's the time?'

'Eight p.m.'

He twisted in the bunk and wound first his right watch and then his left. 'Did Beesley send you?'

'I came because I have fallen in love with you – or, at any rate, with what you might become ...'

'Does that hurt?'

'Yes.'

'And that?'

'Yes.'

'Well, let's get at it, then.'

It was dark when Jerry peeled back the encrusted sheets. Moonlight now came through the porthole. She murmured sleepily and held out her arms to him.

Jerry gave it to her on the point of the chin and fell forward to lie on top of her, breathing hard. He rested for a moment and then slid over her and fell to the floor, rolled and reached out for a rail, pulled himself up and staggered towards the middle of the cabin and kneeled down to pick up her heavy handbag. He opened it with an effort and closed his fingers over the butt of the vibragun. It was his only link with the cellar in Ladbroke Grove.

As his strength returned he sighed. With pleasure, he stood up and looked down at Mitzi. She was stirring.

He glanced at his gun, then at his right watch.

Somewhere a piano began to play.

He slipped into his silks, buckled on his shoulder holster, put the gun into it, and then began to tear up her clothes until he had several long strips of cloth. As he tightened the gag her eyes opened so he turned her over and trussed her up, patting her bottom affectionately.

'So long, Mitzi.' Was it a set-up? he wondered.

He opened the cabin door and went up on deck. The lights of St Paul were on the larboard as the ship moved slowly past the city. On the starboard Minneapolis was in darkness.

'Mr Cornelius, sir!' The whisper came from the bridge. He looked. The ex-chairman of the Arts Council, his worried face pale in the reflected light from the water, hissed at him. 'You shouldn't be on deck alone, sir.'

More in sorrow than in anger, Jerry drew his gun and shook the steward down. He turned at a sound.

Moving towards him from the stern came a fat silhouette. A Remington banged.

'Stop!'

Jerry holstered his gun and leapt for the rail.

Another bang.

'Mr Cornelius! Really! How did you get your gun back?'

'You'll find out. Your bum trouble makes you forget some details, bishop. Cheerio!'

He plunged down in the cold water and began to strike for the bank.

There were a few more bangs but they soon stopped.

Jerry swam as fast as he could because he disliked dark rivers and this tasted particularly foul, so much so that he feared for his suit. He swam along the wharf until he reached some iron steps and climbed out.

A couple of longshoremen ran towards him but he stopped

them in their tracks by waving his gun at them. He looked around.

He was in front of a line of low sheds. Beyond the sheds came the sounds of a busy road. He backed along an alley between two sheds until he came to a high fence. He shook a hole in the fence and stepped down a grassy embankment until he got to the road.

Speeding cars filled all the lanes.

Jerry waved to a cruising police car and it slowed. The car had two cops in it. The one who wasn't driving leaned out of the window. 'What's your trouble, sir?' He grinned at his companion.

'Fell off a boat,' Jerry gasped. 'You gotta help me, boss.'

'Calm down, sonny. How'd you come to fall off of a boat?'

'Yes, sir.'

The cop opened the door and climbed with studied slowness out, pulling a notebook from his tunic pocket. 'You wouldn't be running away from anyone, would you?'

'No, sir.' Jerry rolled his eyes as best he could. 'No, sir!'

'Because we've been having a lot of trouble with runaways of one sort or another just recently.'

'Yes, sir.'

'You got an identity card?'

'A what, boss?'

'An identity card, boy. Everybody's got an identity card unless he's an outlaw or escaper or injun or something.'

'Identity. Nope, sir. I guess I ain't.'

'Uh huh. Then I think . . .'

Jerry lined him up and watched him shake. Then, as his companion began to drag his pistol from its holster, Jerry turned the gun on him and he shook, too.

He stowed them in the back seat as a curious Cadillac slowed down, then he got in, started the car, turned on the siren and got rapidly up to a hundred, heading out of town along Interstate 35E.

By morning his suit had dried nicely and the dirt had fallen off it. He had switched cars twice. Now he was driving a handsome golden Chevrolet Caprice and was on Interstate 90, making for the badlands of South Dakota, having crossed the Missouri at Chamberlain. There weren't many cops about.

The explanation, for what it was worth, was in the two-day-old edition of *The Pioneer Press* he had found in the Caprice. There had been a massive draft of all able-bodied men and women over the age of eighteen. Even those who had previously been designated as performing necessary public offices had been drafted.

At the Totanka Yotanka Motel he stole some gas and was soon in the badlands on a lonely, dusty highway where, at about seven in the evening, he saw the first Sioux.

The war chief was mounted on a black and white pony that had elaborately beaded and painted buckskin trappings. It stood stock still on the rise while its rider gave Jerry's car the once-over.

The warrior was probably an Oglala. He carried a bow-lance decorated with red, white and yellow feathers; on his left arm the round buffalo hide shield had a picture of an eagle surrounded by stars. His bleached, fringed buckskin jacket and leggings were embroidered with coloured beads and shiny red and yellow porcupine quills and his neck was heavy with beads and medallions. His head-dress of curving stag antlers had a feathered train that spread over his pony's rump. There was a knife and a tomahawk at his belt. His high cheek-bones, deep-set eyes, prominent nose and long, thin mouth was the distinctive modern American face. It was in full war-paint, with yellow orange, blue and white bands, circles and triangles.

Raising his bow-lance the chief summoned his war party to join him on the rise. They appeared to be a mixture of Oglalas and Hunkpapas, most of them wearing a great many feathers.

Jerry kept going when he saw the short bows and the bark quivers crammed with arrows, but he knew they'd get him at the next bend.

When he reached the next bend they were waiting for him.

Arrows thudded into the convertible's roof and he heard the Indians' howls as they hurled their mounts towards him at an angle to the highway. The car hit a pony and the war chief fell forward on to the hood, glaring through the windscreen at Jerry who skidded and went off the highway, hit a rock, stepped on the brake, bounced the Indian off the hood on to the ground, wound down the window and drew his vibragun.

The other Sioux lined up along the highway, bows ready, watching to see what he would do as their leader picked himself up and tried to pull his tomahawk from his belt. 'You killed my fucking pony.'

'You put it in front of my fucking car. I had the right of way.'

'Watch your language, schvartze.'

'What are you going to do about it?'

The Indian rubbed his nose and looked around. He straightened the polished bones of his breastplate and slapped the dust off his leggings. 'Besides, we didn't know you was a schvartze. We got no fight with you.'

'I'm not a schvartze.'

'Sure, and I'm not a fucking Oglala.'

Jerry opened the door and got out. 'Are you trying to prove something?'

'MAYBE.' The war chief at last got his tomahawk free and went into a crouch, his eyes narrowing.

Jerry kicked him in the face. He fell over and Jerry picked up the tomahawk. It was very ornamental.

The war chief looked up with an expression of puzzled resignation. 'I wasn't expecting that. You win. What's now?'

'I think we should become blood brothers or something.' Jerry helped him up. 'Isn't that the custom?'

'What the hell if it isn't. It sounds okay to me. We'll have a ceremony at the big council. That's where we're going to now. Iron Mountain.'

'Sounds fine. It's on my way.'

'Great. Baby, we're in this together. We already got a few schvartzes riding with us. Honorary members, I guess. We got to pick up what we can where we can.' He held out his hand. 'I'm Flaming Lance.' He blushed.

Jerry said generously: 'Call me Buffalo Nose.'

Flaming Lance shouted to the others. 'He rides with the Sioux!'

'Hoka hai,' said Jerry.

5. The Game's the Same, the Players Change, but the Stakes are Still Your Guns

During the next couple of weeks their numbers grew and they raided several farmhouses on their way through Wyoming, Colorado and Utah. Jerry wore a sparsely feathered war bonnet, blue and yellow paint, bone bow, quiver of arrows, hunting knife and a tomahawk, but he hadn't given up his silk suit. He rode a pinto pony and was beginning to regret it.

Near Iron Mountain they waited. Then from the West came the Bannock, the Shoshoni, the Paviosto, the Pyute. From the East came the Osage, the Pawnee and the Omaha. From the North came the Cree, the Blackfoot, the Gros Ventre, the Flathead, the Assinboine. And from the South came the Cheyenne, the Kiowa and the Comanche.

The councils began. All night there were dances and drumming, pipe-smoking and wampum-passing, and the medicine men cast their bones or necromantically raised up the ghosts of the great dead braves who appeared in the red smoke of the fires – Geronimo, Red Sleeve, Chief Joseph, Osceola, Cornplanter, Red Jacket, Rain-in-the-Face, Red Cloud, Sitting Bull, Crow, Black Kettle, Crazy Horse, Roman Nose, Little Wolf, White Antelope – all the heroes of the High Plains, the forests, the valleys and the mountains. And during the day there was the Sun Dance, or the dances of the warrior societies, or the women's dances, like the White Buffalo Dance. And they would listen to their Paramount Chiefs as they spoke of the glory that would soon be theirs as all the Indian Nations united and claimed the land that was theirs by right.

Jerry caught up with his sleep as best he could. He had mingled blood with Flaming Lance and felt he had done his bit. The council grounds were becoming a bit crowded and smelly as thousands more Navahos, Chiricahuas, Mescaleros, Wichitas, Chickasaws, Shawnees, Kickapoos, Santees, Cayuses, Modocs and Nez Perces flooded in.

It was time to be off.

He left unostentatiously in an old Thunderbird that had

brought the Paramount Chief of the Choctaws. He made it to St George by morning and drove through the rubble. Scalped corpses were everywhere.

Soon he was on Interstate 15, heading for Las Vegas where he hoped he might pick up a plane that would get him to San Francisco.

He was becoming extremely concerned for his patients.

6. Live, Work, Fish and Hunt in Nature's Wonderland!

Las Vegas was quiet in the afternoon glare. The signs flashed to a steady, soothing rhythm that blended with the sounds of the one-armed bandits and the blackjack tables. Las Vegas was one of those sleepy towns where nobody bothered you much as long as you didn't make trouble. It had all the old virtues of rural American life. Jerry felt at peace here. He made for Circus Circus and wondered if Murphy still owned it.

He went inside and began to cross the vast hall filled with gaming tables. A few old people were playing, a few performers were on the high wire above the hall, but nobody noticed him as he located Murphy's office and went in.

Murphy seemed pleased to see him.

'Jerry! What brings you to civilization?'

'I thought you might like to know that the tribes are massing. It looks like war.'

'We don't need to worry about a few Indians, Jerry. The army'll look after them.'

'The army seems to be busy elsewhere.'

'Why should they want to attack us?'

Eugene Murphy had known Jerry in London. Ex-president-turned-motion-picture-star-turned-casino-owner, Murphy had a battered, cancerous face and a big cigar.

'They're attacking everything,' said Jerry.

'What are they riled about?'

'Most everything or nothing in particular. You know the Indians.'

Murphy nodded. 'Well, I'll bear it in mind. Is that why you came to Vegas?'

'I came to borrow a plane. I lost mine out there.'

'Sure. You can have your pick. I've got a lovely little LTV C-150A tiltwing turboprop that should suit you fine. Have something to eat and then we'll go and take a look at her. What d'you say?'

'Sounds fine.'

'Great! I bet you're glad to be somewhere you can put your feet up. All that trouble. All that burning. Washington, Atlanta, Kansas City, Philadelphia, Salt Lake City, Houston. I sometimes wonder if it's worth it, Jerry.' Murphy poured them both large glasses of rye. 'And it's not good for business, either. I can tell you that for nothing. You must have come through the place. Not that I'm complaining. Not yet.'

Jerry peeled off his war-bonnet. 'I think they'll make for Carson City and take over the mint first. They were still in council when I left.'

'I'm part Indian myself, you know,' Murphy said proudly.

7. Cops Who are Hell on Pillheads

Jerry climbed into the cockpit of the LTV C-150A and ran his fingers over the controls with a sigh of relief. He settled himself and switched on. Slowly the wings tilted upwards and the propellers sang.

Jerry sat back and took her up.

She rose neatly into the air and at five hundred feet he tilted the wings forward and headed, at a comfortable 350 mph, for California.

As he flew over the Sierra Nevadas he saw that they were black with riders. A Mayday message came in on the radio. It was Sacramento.

'This is General Partridge, Sacramento Control Tower.'

'Come in Partridge, Sacramento.'

'We're completely surrounded. I've hardly got a man left. We can't get a message through for reinforcements. Will you relay a message?'

'What's the problem?'

'The problem! Indians is the problem. They're howling round and round and round. Fire arrows ...'

'How long can you hang on?'

'Another hour. We need paratroopers. A regiment at least. Half the tower's on fire. Can you get through to Hollywood?'

'I don't think so.'

'Well, get through to someone. There must be a thousand of the devils out there at least. My head's spinning. Round and round. Nobody warned me.'

'It's a fast world, general.'

'No kidding.'

'I'm on my way to San Francisco. I'll inform the authorities when I arrive.'

'If we hadn't had guerilla experience, we wouldn't be here now. It's Dien Bien Phu all over again.'

'That's the way it goes. Over and out, general.'

Jerry could see the blue Pacific. He began to hum.

*

Jerry brought the plane down over the mellow ruins of Berkeley and headed for the recently built Howard Johnson's where he had a large steak with all the trimmings and a Quadruple Pineapple Astonisher with hot fudge sauce topped with grated nuts. It set him up. He left one of Murphy's thousand dollar bills under his plate and began the long walk to the bridge. The bay was blue, the bridge beautiful and the distant city had almost died down. A few buildings were still standing, a few reconnaissance copters hung about in the sky but most of them were heading back to the Hollywood base, not the Greater American operations centre.

An old man joined Jerry as he reached the bridge. 'Mind if I walk along with you a taste, son?' He wore a dingy brown fedora and dirty overalls and he had a cheroot between his wrinkled lips. 'Going in for a loved one?'

'Something like that.' The bridge swayed, Jerry looked down at the boats leaving the bay. Most of them were cruisers from the ruined port.

'I hail from Kansas. I was on my way to join up in LA, but then the truck broke down. Thought I'd do some fruit-picking instead.'

Jerry stopped and peered through the bars. He recognized the *Teddy Bear*. She was going full steam and she was loaded with patients; he saw some of them staring up from the forward hold just before the hatches were battened. Beesley must have moved the yacht overland in a hurry. Now they were heading out.

'There's a lot of fruit to pick,' said the old man. 'So I hear.'

Jerry sighed.

'I'll be seeing you,' he said, and he jumped, swung through the struts, poised, dived, hit the salty water not three feet from the yacht, sank, somersaulted, struck for the surface, saw above him the keel, the churning propellers and grabbed the rope that trailed in the foam, hauling himself up the side.

When he climbed aboard he had his vibragun in his hand and Bishop Beesley and Mitzi had a nasty shock when they saw him.

'That was just a warning.' Jerry smiled apologetically. 'I seem to be in and out of water all the time.' He waved them

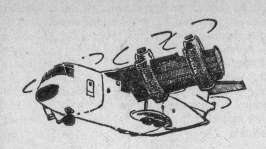

towards the rail over which he'd climbed. 'It's your turn for a dip now.'

'Good heavens, Mr Cornelius! This is piracy!'

'Well, I see it another way, bishop. After all, it's my crew.'

'That's a moot point, sir!'

'Jerry.' Mitzi's eyes were full of adoration. 'Let me come with you. I'll be . . .'

'I'd like that, Mitzi, but I have to remain impartial at the moment. You've used up so much of my time, do you see. You know how it is.'

She tripped to the side, pulled her tight, white skirt over her creamy thighs and straddled the gleaming brass rail.

With a wave she disappeared.

'Now you, bishop.'

'A boat, at very least ...'

'Come along, now.'

The bishop moved reluctantly and looked down at the sparkling water. 'When I asked you for a lift ...'

'Don't make me feel guilty.'

'I shouldn't think it would take me ...'

'Bishop.'

'A bag of provender. A Bounty bar?'

'Not even a coffee cream.'

'I don't like coffee creams.' Blowing like a great white whale, Bishop Beesley heaved himself over the rail. Somewhere a building toppled and crashed.

Jerry walked up and pushed him on his way. With a yell the bishop whirled his corpulent arms and fell on the water. He lay there, bobbing up and down in the yacht's wake, his arms and legs waving gently, his red mouth opening and closing, his bulging eyes staring at Jerry in pained outrage. Mitzi appeared, shaking water from her hair, and began to tow the bishop shorewards.

'Bye, bye, bishop. It's like a game of dominoes in many ways.'

The bishop honked pathetically.

Jerry climbed up the companionway to the bridge and checked his charts and instruments, plotting his course.

Within half an hour they were bound for Sumatra where the organization had an emergency Reclamation Centre, and Greater America had disappeared below the horizon.

3. SECOND OPERATION

The Dream

Four years ago I dreamed that I
stood in a room behind, and to the left of,
a young man I did not know. He was
younger than me. On his left, but in front
of us, my brother, and beside him
stood an old man whom I did not
recognize. On our right, two large cream-
painted doors were closing. I thought that
my brother and this other man were in
some way assessing this younger man, who
I felt was either my husband or my
intended husband. Since then, I have
without any doubt met this young man.
The dream is troubling me, as I fail to
understand its meaning. Never before have
I dreamed so clearly of something so far in
the future.

The Meaning

We may accept the above as a good
example of what is called precognitive
dreaming. Instances of dreaming ahead of
time crop up fairly often and some of them
get on to this page. As to what the brother
and the old man are doing, that comes
under a different head altogether. The
earliest objects of a girl child's physical
affection are her father and her brother.
Any later male attachment is a result of
these early, though unlocalized, sex

objects. The question the reader is asking
in her dream is how far the later object
of affection stands up to the early ideal of
childhood. The result rests with the
dreamer's own nature. The old man is
a father symbol; the closing doors
represent the flight of time.

Dream Meanings, *Prediction*, March 1969

OUTER SPACE: IN THE BEGINNING,
A BIG BANG

Fantastic things are being discovered in outer space. Some astronomers believe they have located cosmic bodies of cataclysmic force that might indicate a primeval Big Bang. And a hiss located in outer space may be an echo of this explosive Creation, coming from thousands of millions of light years ago. Next week, in an exciting new series, we explore the new ideas which may lead to a complete overhaul of our thinking about the universe and our place in it.

Observer Colour Magazine, January 26th 1969

1. UFOs are Unfriendly, Up to No Good, and Some of Them are Truly Dangerous

A quick trip to the cellar, then Jerry moved easy in soft browns and yellows and a gold silk tie out into the mellow sunlight of an early autumn in Ladbroke Grove, on his way to Chelsea.

Kings Road was a healthy step away.

He strolled along, savouring the day, swinging his sonic cane and listening to the music in the handle, turned down Elgin Crescent, shaded by old oaks, and trod the length of Clarendon Road until he came to Holland Park Avenue with its tall trees and its huge, hollow, empty houses.

Pulled by two Shetland ponies, a red and green baker's cart moved slowly through the falling leaves. The lean driver stretched on his seat in the soft warmth of the day, listening to the lazy drone of distant aircraft. Jerry stopped and bought a bun.

'It's a mild sort of day,' said the baker.

'Not bad.' Jerry bit his bun. 'How's the wife?'

'Not so dusty.'

'Finished your round?'

'For what it's worth. Very little bread, of course. Just the eclairs and custard tarts and stuff.'

'I suppose it's for the best.'

'Wouldn't have it otherwise.'

Jerry headed for the park. His cane played *The Fool on the Hill*.

A few children ran about in Holland Park as he passed through. An old man fed the peacocks and pigeons and guinea fowl from a big tub of peanuts at his belt. Jerry paused by Holland House and looked at its white façade, but the Elizabethan mansion was silent so he kept going until he reached the cricket pitch and the burnt-out skeleton of the Commonwealth Institute that faced Kensington High Street where the traffic moved slowly.

He had a feeling in his bones.

On the corner of Earls Court Road, he climbed into his parked Maybach Zeppelin convertible, pushed back the top to let the breeze get to his hair, drove rapidly towards Chelsea and stopped outside *The Purple Parrot* where he had arranged to meet Spiro Koutrouboussis to discuss the past, present and future over lunch.

The lobby of the club was hung with gilded cages full of mynah birds, canaries and cockatoos who called to each other in several languages and dialects. The receptionist, dressed in elaborate quills, looked like a Polynesian chief in ceremonial robes. She smiled at him. 'Your table's ready, Mr Cornelius. Your friend's in the Linnet Room.'

Spiro Koutrouboussis sat by himself on a stool by the bar, staring pensively at a cage of sulky wrens. A thrush perched on his curly black hair, a Marguerita lay between his well-scrubbed hands. 'Ah, Cornelius.'

'Sorry if I'm late. I had rather a rough time in the States.'

'I told you so.'

Jerry sniffed.

'That Karen von Krupp – she trapped you. I knew she would. You never listen ...'

The thrush began to sing. Koutrouboussis brushed at it absently but it dug its claws in.

'It was an experience.' Jerry ordered a Pernod. 'Nothing like experience.'

'The *time* lost!'

'That's something you can never do anything about. Come now, Koutrouboussis. Let's see a smile, eh?'

'Cornelius. We are in danger. Our whole project is in danger – *your* project, after all. If you have double-crossed ...'

Jerry reached for the menu on the bar. 'What have we got?'

'The duck's very good today,' said Koutrouboussis 'So I'm told. Or the Chicken Apollinaire.'

'Too heavy for me. I'll start with *paté de foie*, I think.' Jerry stroked the tip of his nose. 'I miss the food. Still ...'

'Is Karen von Krupp out of the picture now?'

'I should imagine so.'

'Well, I suppose you were successful, essentially. But there's still Beesley. Particularly under the circumstances.'

'Which circumstances are those?'

'President Boyle has increased the military advisors. There are three million on the Continent, seeking out certain fifth column elements.'

'Surely nobody's worried.'

'Not about that. Nobody but the Three Presidents, anyway. And maybe Israel. You heard what happened yesterday? A fleet of Israeli helicopters landed in the Vatican City and arrested the Pope. Admittedly, they had a lot of aggravation.'

'I've been a bit out of touch.'

'I'm not blaming you for that.'

They walked into the restaurant. It had been converted from an old orangery and its pillars were covered in vines, its windows looking out on to a white paved courtyard with a Regency fountain in which sparrows splashed.

Jerry ordered his hors d'oeuvre and chose roast quail as his main dish. They decided to drink Blue Nun.

'I think the machine should be found, you know.' Koutrouboussis chewed his chicken. 'After all, we're not in a very strong position without it, are we? Our chances are slim.'

'I don't much fancy the Shifter at this stage.' Jerry picked up a little leg.

'You might not have to go into it. We've got something of a lead. Does the name – ?' Koutrouboussis choked on an asparagus spear. 'Does the name,' he took a sip of his Liebfraumilch, 'Gordon mean anything to you?'

'Flash Gordon?'

'Gordon Gavin?'

'That's right.' Jerry nipped at a quail's breast. 'He has twenty-two offences behind him. For flashing.'

'Ah. Well, be that as it may, he got in contact with me a little while ago. He'd heard about our conversion scheme.'

'So he's at a centre.'

'Not yet. You know how timid these people are. He made an appointment but didn't keep it. Then he phoned again to say he had a message for you from a gentleman concerning an invention of yours that got lost during a test run. The machine, obviously.'

'I've lost a lot of inventions.'

'I'm sure he meant the machine. It could be our salvation, Cornelius.'

'Get away.'

2. Ignore Advice to Strip at High Speed

Koutrouboussis crossed the street heavily and entered the gates of the Pheasantry where he had an apartment. Jerry followed him down the crazy paving between the crumbling statues and into the dark hall full of varnished doors and unseen fluttering wings.

They went along silent corridors, across quiet courtyards and up stairs until they were deep in the Victorian complex. Koutrouboussis stopped by a door on a second floor balcony overlooking a rock garden full of finches. The door's wood had been stripped and a thin yellow undercoat had been laid on the top half.

'Here we are.'

They went into a sunlit studio. On the raised door to the right stood a brass bed with a large, loud, enamelled bird of paradise as its headboard. The bed also had a Turkish counterpane in dark red, yellow and blue.

The raised floor to the left had deep white cupboards containing Koutrouboussis's sink, stove and supplies.

An Old Gold fitted carpet covered the floor and the steps; by the far wall a large light screen was full of flowing colours that frequently changed shape.

In the corners, close to the ceiling, were four quad speakers. In the middle of the floor kneeled two girls wearing lace and feathers, pale make-up, lots of big rings, and richly decorated eyes.

As the girls looked softly at him, Jerry remembered them.

'Hello, Jerry,' murmured Barbara the Groupie.

'Maureen and Barbara are staying with me for a bit.' Koutrouboussis loosened his tie. 'They're between groups at the moment.'

Maureen had honey-coloured hair and Barbara had chestnut-coloured hair; they stood gracefully up and went to the kitchen where they collected two tins and brought them back.

Maureen put an old Zoot Money record on the deck. The sound came softly through and the light screen shifted its shapes and colours.

Barbara kneeled to make some cigarettes. She took the ingredients from the tins with her delicate fingers and rolled fat, full fags. She lit two and handed one to Jerry and the other to Koutrouboussis. The men sat down on the ostrich plume cushions and smoked.

Maureen came back and kneeled beside Barbara; she drew on her cigarette with vague dignity. Then both girls tilted their impassive faces and directed their inturned eyes at the skylight until someone should ask for something.

'Now if it wasn't for the beans that came out the can, the peas, the beef, the rice and the spam, you can get going down to the grocer's store, really I couldn't eat no more. Let me tell you, my wife – now she can't cook and if I thought she could I wouldn't bother, but all she can do is fuss and holler, she don't even know him to boil water,' sang Zoot Money.

'Nineteen sixty-five.' Koutrouboussis took a long pull. 'So long, long, long ...'

'If you leave me, I'll go crazy.'

Jerry smiled back reminiscently at Maureen the Groupie who smiled back, sharing the secret that only kindness made them keep.

'Jump back, baby, jump back ...'

Koutrouboussis lay down and closed his face.

Maureen's warm lips framed the words as she and Jerry looked matily into each other's eyes: ('Sweet little rock and roller ...')

It was too much for Jerry.

He got up and grasped Maureen and Barbara by their small, soft hands and led them across the Old Gold carpet, up the three steps to the bed with its bird of paradise and began to pile the lace and feathers and rings they handed him. They were so fine and their style was so nice; and their agile, graceful, malleable bodies moved to their mutual pleasure.

When the record was finished, Barbara went and put on another. It was Zoot Money's *Zoot!*

Jerry looked across to the middle of the room.

Koutrouboussis's eyes were alive in a frozen, fading frame. 'Pigs.'

3. The New RM Top 50 Chart Explained

Jerry, Maureen and Barbara left the Pheasantry and went in Jerry's car to the Ball Room in Wardour Street, Soho, where, in a spot that shifted through all the shades of blue, Sneaky Jack Slade whined wildly his signature tune, played on his smooth sitar.

'I'm the sneaky guy, don't deny my name. Yes, I'm the sneaky guy, don't deny my name,' he sang.

When Sneaky saw the new arrivals come in he scuttled off the little stage to be followed by Jonni Jane in platinum wig and rosepetal suit.

Jonni's hands flung themselves about. 'Now it's time for our newest, bluest – let me introduce you – twelve or eight to the bar – to the bombshock blues of the junkiest, funkiest, wailingest picker of the year – get ready – he's coming – it's Clapham – George – *Foulsham*!' Jonni trolled off and on came Clapham George to play his latest composition, *Ma Belly's Fulla Sour Milk*.

'Mean ol' UD, brought sour milk to me. Oh, that mean ol' UD, brought sour milk to me ...'

Leaving Maureen and Barbara by the Coca Cola stand, Jerry went to look for Lionel Himmler, the proprietor.

He found him, all sorrow and shit, in his little office behind the bar.

'And what brings you out in the daytime, Mr Cornelius?' Lionel lifted a glass of Bull's Blood to his pale lips. 'Not a blunt needle, I hope.'

'How's business, Lionel?'

'We're going over to strip shows more. You've got to get the customers from the suburbs, you see. Out of the Stockbroker Belt into the Suspender Belt, eh?' A cigar reared in his mouth.

'Soho isn't what it was.'

'Let me be the judge of that, Mr Cornelius.'

'I felt like working.'

'It's your mortgage.'

Jerry opened a dark brown cupboard and took out his Martin 206. He checked it and turned it.

'Sorry about the dust,' said Lionel.

His guitar under his arm, Jerry walked back into the room. Clapham George had gone and a stripper towelled herself in the strobelight. Jerry flickered to a table, sat down and ordered scotch and milk.

Maureen and Barbara brought their Cokes over and joined him. He felt happy with them, but they all knew the scene was patched.

When the stripper went backstage, Jerry played *Dutch Schultz* and then sang *Back Door Man* and Lionel came out to play the Hammond and Jerry plugged in on the stage and things moved a little as the audience went and only Maureen and Barbara, two old, old ladies, listened as Jerry mournfully finished with *My Baby Rocks Me*, which got them all going, so they left.

Jerry blew a kiss to Lionel. He didn't notice. He was playing a John Patton number, probably *Fat Judy*.

Off they went. Through the cold grease of the crowd on the pavement and down the street to where his car, a 1935 Phantom III Continental Rolls-Royce with its involved V-12 engine and its independent front suspension and its fixtures of the purest silver, including the radiator, was parked.

'Maybe it should have been a Shadow,' said Barbara giving Jerry's arm a friendly hug. 'Or is that perverse?'

The girls climbed in the back with the Martin and Jerry started the car.

Wardour Street, all frozen brightlights and vague expressions, led to Shaftesbury Avenue, walled by brown shops, to Piccadilly Circus, and its green spot.

Soon Jerry was out of all that, driving down Pall Mall, round the palace, along beside the park, past the Victory Arch, into Knightsbridge, bowling along, singing a song, while the girls, huddled in each other's arms, fell asleep.

The music was going.

Koutrouboussis was right. He had to find the machine. He would drop the groupies off at the Pheasantry, get the whereabouts of Gordon Gavin and make an early start in the morning.

4. My Husband is a 'Speed Freak'

Jerry rode the 750cc MZ motorbike straight down the middle of Hammersmith Road. The hog began to hammer as it reached 130.

Jerry's milk-white hair stood out straight behind him, his black silks were pasted to his body, his visor threatened to buckle as he leaned and took the roundabout and throttled down to a comfortable ton when he neared the Cromwell Road Extension and passed a funeral procession.

Three Austin Princesses followed the hearse, their debased lines and lumpen finish offering some loathsome insult to the coffin's contents.

Lying forward on the tank, with his arms stretched out to grasp the chopper's low racing bars, Jerry weaved in front of the Princesses in a dance that was at once graceful and obscene.

The gesture made, he accelerated again and screamed towards Brentford Market.

The Austin Princess was bad for his cool.

He turned into Kew Bridge Road, leapt over the bridge and headed along Kew Green for the big main gates, designed by Decimus Burton and erected in 1848, of the Royal Botanic Gardens. He went through the wrought iron gates that bore the golden Royal Crest, and reduced his speed to seventy, passing the John Nash Aroid House, the Chambers Orangery, the Filmy Fern House, his bike leaving a churned scar across the autumn lawns until it hit Broad Walk and zoomed through the fresh, early morning air towards the Burton Palm House that glistened, all glass and girders, by the Rose Garden, roared between the Australian House and the Temperate House, gunned through flower beds and lawns, wove between the quiet cedars and skidded to a stop outside the 163 ft Red Pagoda that overlooked the cedars.

The metal plates on each of the pagoda's ten roofs reflected the sun, as did the glass domes that covered the bronze dragons at each corner of each of the octagonal roofs, exactly as they had been placed in 1761 by Sir William Chambers on Princess Augusta's approval.

Jerry let his hog fall and shielded his eyes to peer upward.

There in the shadows of the sixth storey balcony stood a figure which, as he watched, came and leaned over the rail. The figure was dressed in a long, dirty raincoat buttoned to the neck.

It could only be Flash Gordon.

Jerry opened the door and began to climb the central iron staircase that wound up between the bare floors of varnished oak planks. Dust sparkled in the sunlight slanting through the dirty windows.

As he reached the sixth floor, Flash climbed through an open window and stood limply waiting for Jerry to approach.

The large, brown, shallow eyes, set in the red, unhealthy face, stared shiftily at the silk suit, and the blotched fingers

stroked the buttons of his mackintosh as if the urge to undo them would get the better of him at any moment.

Below the raincoat Jerry saw a pair of thick, grey socks and boots heavy with mud and blakeys.

'Er, how do, Mr Cornelius, er.' Flash moved his thick lips in a flabby smile.

'Good morning, Gordon. Kew's a bit off your usual manor, isn't it?'

Flash brightened up. 'Ah, well. I'm fond of plants, you see, Mr Cornelius. I had a little garden. I do a little gardening. I'd like a little shrubbery. A little greenhouse. I'm fond of plants. All kinds. I look after these now, as best I can. There's no one else will. That's the state of this little country.'

'And it's handy.'

'Very handy.' As Flash dropped his lids over his suddenly heating pupils his hands went convulsively into his pockets. 'And warm. Winter's coming,' he whispered. Then he cleared his throat. 'But I need a good bit of oil. And oil doesn't grow on trees. Well ... not on most ∴ .. trees.' Avoiding Jerry's eyes Flash moved to the staircase and began to climb down. 'Shall us?'

'It is a bit exposed here,' agreed Jerry unpleasantly as he followed Flash down.

They walked along the golden Cedar Vista towards the distant Australian House.

'It's spring in Australia, of course,' Flash murmured.

'I wouldn't count on it. Not these days.'

'I suppose not, no.'

Flash took a key from his pocket and opened the door. They went into the hot, bright atmosphere and strolled among the eucalyptus, banksias, Kangaroo Paw, Sturt's Desert Pea, mimosa and acacia.

'You told our Mr Koutrouboussis you had some information about some stolen property,' Jerry said as they paused to admire the purple flowers of a rhododendron.

'Perfectly correct.'

'Hard or soft information?'

Flash gave him a startled look. 'Er, hard, er.'

'And you want a transplant job in return?'

'Ah, well, that's it, isn't it? No. You see, I'm happy here. I like the plants and they like me. And I can move about in them, can't I, waiting for the visitors?'

'So you can.'

'Therefore, Mr Cornelius, by and large, that problem's settled. Over and done with. It's a different problem. I'd give you the info for nothing, you know that. For old time's sake. But I've got to have the oil, you see.'

'Well, we could guarantee you a regular supply. Oil's one thing we had a bit of foresight on.'

'That's what I understand.'

'And, of course, we'd have a guarantee that way, wouldn't we?'

'That's right. If my info's duff, you stop the supply. I hope it isn't duff, though.' Flash looked anxiously at his Kangaroo Paw. 'I wish you hadn't done that to my lawn.'

'I wasn't to know, Flash.'

'Fair enough. It'll grow over. That's something I've got to face, sooner or later. There'll be a good deal of growing over.'

'It won't be a bad thing.'

'I didn't say it was. But it's *different*, isn't it, I mean?'

A squadron of low-flying Northrop F-5A Freedom Fighters made the glass buzz in the frames. Flash looked up and shook his head. 'There's been a lot of parachuting going on,' he said. 'Over Barnes way mostly. You should see what *they've* done to the grass and the trees on the common.'

'They've got our interests at heart,' said Jerry.

'But what about the little saplings and that!'

'You'll have to make some sacrifices, Flash.'

Warm tears dropped from Gordon's eyes. 'Well, I used to like Barnes Common. Sorry, Mr Cornelius, but I did. That's where I first met you, wasn't it?'

'That info you were on about,' said Jerry.

'Oh, yes. Yes. Just a minute.' Flash's hand moved in his raincoat pocket and eventually emerged with a scrap of paper. 'The swine.'

He handed Jerry the piece of paper. 'It is a deal, isn't it, Mr Cornelius?'

Jerry looked at the paper. 'It's a deal. Where did you get this?'

'Off the bloke that wrote it.'

'That bugger,' said Jerry. 'Would you believe it?'

'It's all go, isn't it?' said Flash.

Jerry looked at the piece of paper again:

'He said he'd made an appointment for you. Buckingham Palace. This afternoon.' Flash stroked a eucalyptus leaf. 'Is that all right?'

'It'll have to do.'

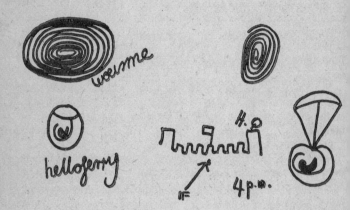

Cut One

Frightened mothers welcome the avenging police.

Police in Rio de Janeiro and São Paulo were tired of seeing criminals get away scot free. So a few of them organised 'death squads' – which operate only during the coppers' off-duty hours.

So far the deaths of more than 100 criminals have been attributed to the Rio squad. The bodies were stamped with a skull-and-cross-bones, which is the trade mark of the killer cops.

The São Paulo squad is believed to consist of nine officers, five of them university-educated. Their grudge is the abolition of the death penalty in Brazil and the lack of adequate police facilities.

One squad member, who preferred to be nameless, said: 'We were fed up with going around with our hands tied. We decided to use unconventional methods.'

Honest people among the ten million who live in the two cities welcome the unorthodox justice.

One frightened mother wrote to a local newspaper: 'It is good to know we are being protected.'

The men marked for death are those considered habitual criminals by the squads.

Many are drug traffickers. The squads seek maximum publicity, feeling that this will be a deterrent to crime.

The official police stations receive regular calls from a squad 'public relations officer', who reveals where the latest body can be found.

Titbits, February 1st 1969

1. Ecological Effects of the Viet Nam War

Jerry pulled his Phantom VI up outside the gates of Buckingham Palace and lowered the window as two sergeants of the 5th Marine Division in the modified uniforms of the Grenadiers, complete with helmets and horsehair plumes, came to check him over.

'I've an appointment with Frank Cornelius,' Jerry told them.

He was wearing his wide-brimmed lilac hat, with his hair knotted under it. His midnight-blue shirt was trimmed in matching lace and his toreador trousers were in an even deeper blue. Around his waist was a wide patent leather belt with a huge brass buckle and a holster holding his vibragun. A flowing yellow bandanna had been tied around his throat.

The sergeants tried to keep their faces expressionless as they inspected his papers, but their lips trembled.

'Wait here, sir.' One of the sergeants brushed at his new moustache and went and spoke to a man who stood in the shadows of the main entrance to the palace building.

The other sergeant rested his hand on the roof of Jerry's car and watched his companion intently until he emerged from the shadows and waved. The sergeant slammed the flat of his hand on the roof and Jerry drove through into the courtyard.

The first sergeant ran up to the car, his sword and forty-five slapping against his white buckskins.

'I'll park your car, sir.'

'Don't bother.' Jerry got out and locked the Phantom VI. 'I'll leave it here, I think.'

'We can't do that. Cars outside headquarters are forbidden. They ruin the view. Sir.'

Jerry pointed up at the flagstaff on the roof of the palace. 'I see General Cumberland's in residence.'

'Yes, sir.'

'It's a proud banner.'

Jerry walked into the hall and gave his card to a dapper

lieutenant who placed it on a silver tray and bore it up the staircase, passing the portraits of Elizabeth I, James I, Charles I, Charles II, James II, William III, Mary II, Anne, George I, George II, George III, George IV, William IV, Victoria, Edward VII, George V, Edward VIII, George VI, Elizabeth II, Helen and Ulysses Washington Cumberland (C-in-C; US Defence Forces, Western Europe) who had occupied the building after Helen had left to run a small riding school in Guildford, Surrey. The most recent of the portraits were by Aldridge, the last true Court Painter, in the mouth-and-foot manner that he had made so markedly his own.

Jerry admired the old-fashioned luxury, the archaic splendour of the guards who had stood at attention with drawn sabres at every door.

'They certainly have dash.' He nodded at the guards as the lieutenant returned.

The lieutenant eyed him up and down. 'Major Cornelius is ready to see you. This way.'

They climbed the plush and gold staircase until they reached the second floor and walked between the panelled walls and bad Romneys until they came to a white door with panel decorations picked out in black; the name MAJOR FRANK CORNELIUS, *Special Aide, C-in-C*, inscribed in red, and two splendid Royal Marine US Marine Grenadiers on either side. Their swords clashed as they ceremoniously barred the portal then returned their weapons to the slope.

The lieutenant knocked on the door.

A faint but unmistakable Afrikaaner accent answered: 'Come.'

The lieutenant saluted and marched off. Jerry opened the door and walked into a room decorated and furnished entirely in a style as ugly as anything by the Adam Bros.

Frank stood by the fussy fireplace looking at a little lyre clock that was of the German fake Directoire variety but quite pretty. He was dressed in the sharply cut uniform of a major in the US 8th Airborne, one hand in his pocket, one arm on the mantelpiece. He looked very pale and his black hair was clipped close to his shoulders. He smiled at Jerry.

'Long time no see, old chap.'

'You've been out in South Afrika, then.'

'Good for the constitution, Jerry.'

'Or reconstitution.'

Frank laughed loudly. 'Good old Jerry!'

'I wish you wouldn't keep using that word. You seem to be doing well for yourself. How's Mum?'

'It's a mission. I heard she was fine.'

'I saw Mr Gavin. I gather you have some idea of the whereabouts of a piece of property I own.'

'Your invention, you mean.'

'You could put it that way.'

'Well, I haven't got it here, you realize.'

'Where would it be?'

'Let's discuss it later. Time for refreshment first?' Frank touched a bell and a ravaged girl with long chestnut hair came through a side door, 'This is my secretary. Do you know her? Rose Barrie, my brother Jerry. Rose is a civilian auxiliary.' Frank smiled. 'They call you Bombhead Rose, don't they, Rose?' He winked at Jerry. 'Rose knows ...'

Rose smoothed her cherry dress and raised a hand to her garish face. 'Wh ... ?'

'Something to cheer us up, Rose. Good gal, eh?'

Rose went away again.

'She got smacked for speeding,' Frank said. 'But she's my type. You know. I couldn't let her down.'

'You're too good.'

'It's too sweet.'

Rose returned with a white tray on which various bottles, ampoules and instruments were laid.

'Now – let's see,' said Frank. His hand hovered over the tray. 'Anything you fancy, old boy?'

'You go ahead. Unless you've got anything in blue.'

'Rose had the last of the rozzers last night, didn't you, Rose?'

'Y ...'

'She'll tell you. Nothing in blue.'

'Then I'll let it go.'

'As long as you're sure.' Frank picked up an ampoule with the fingertips of his left hand, a needle with the fingertips of his right. 'I've been experimenting too, you know, in my own field. Something that might even interest you, though I know

168

you haven't my obsession with chemistry. A synthesized DNA, with something added.' Frank rolled back his well-cut sleeve and applied the needle. He smacked his lips. 'Tasty. The trouble is, I found, that it's virtually impossible to manufacture in large doses. With your physics and technical know-how, we could be in business.'

'You shouldn't diversify too much, Frank.'

'That's rich advice from you, old man!'

'Besides, it's not a lot to do with my work. Not if you mean transfusions.'

'Transfusions are what I had in mind. A little from that source, a little from this, mix 'em together and see what happens.'

'Schitzy!'

'Quite.'

'But it still isn't my scene. Now, if you could hand over the machine. Or maybe let me know where ...'

'Ah. Well, you see, it's Rose that knows where it is. She told me all about it the other day, didn't you, Rose?'

'I ...'

'It was a vision of some kind, I believe.'

'I ... wish ... I ...'

'Anyway, I checked her out.'

'I ... wish ... I ...'

'And she was right.'

'I ... wish ... I ... was ...'

'So I got in touch with you.'

'I ... wish ... I ... was ... pretty ...'

'So it's around here somewhere is it?' Jerry frowned at Rose. 'In London, I mean?'

'I ... wish ... I ... was ... pretty ... again.'

'Oh, it's in London, old sport.' Frank smiled, turned Rose round and pushed her towards the door. 'That's why I contacted you. I mean, there wouldn't be much time, would there? The way things are working out.'

'You mean ...'

'The Op, old son. The rationalization programme. That's why my boss and I are here, naturally. There's a conference of all European commanders ...' he checked one of his watches ... 'in about ten minutes. General Cumberland has taken emergency measures already, but I don't think they'll contain anything for very long. Berlin, Geneva, Luxembourg are now negative threats and I expect reports on Helsinki and Milan any moment.'

'Bombed?'

'Out of their *minds*, old bean!'

There was a knock on the door.

'Come.'

The lieutenant entered and drew himself up in a salute. 'Sir. The native commanders are in the conference room. The general hoped you'd entertain them until he can make it.'

'Of course. Well, Jerry, if you'll ask Rose for anything you need ... I'll be back in a little while. Take it easy. You look beside yourself!'

'I wish I were.'

'Chin up.' Frank, one hand on the butt of his own neatly stashed needle-gun, struck off towards the door. 'Wise yourself up to the situation, if you like.'

He pulled a cord as he left and the wall over the fireplace glowed and became a map. 'I never forget, you see. You taught me how to do that.'

Jerry glanced at the bright relief map on which little spots of light flickered where cities had been. It was a bit of a bore. He wondered if you could change the channel.

2. Gallagher to Form Label in Thrust Overseas by MCA

Jerry found a button and pushed it.

The map gave way to a scene somewhere in the palace; evidently the conference room. At the long table sat the generals and the field marshals of every European country (with the exception of the Three Republics and the one or two who were still having trouble with the Israelis). They chatted cheerfully among themselves, looking up when Frank, his seamed face set in a smile, came in.

'Gentlemen. I am Major Frank Cornelius, the general's special aide in the European Theatre. Please call me Frank.'

He put down a slim file on the table and took his place near the top. 'General Cumberland regrets he has been delayed, but will join us shortly. In the meantime,' he spreads his hands, 'I'm here to answer any minor questions you might like to put.'

The Bohemian field marshal cleared his thin throat.

'Field Marshal Lobkowitz?' said Frank.

'I was wondering if you could give us a brief run-down on which areas have been – um –'

'Depersonnelized.'

'Ah. Yes.'

'Capitals – Helsinki, Berlin, Geneva, Luxembourg, Vienna. Major conurbations – Milan, Munich, Strassbourg . . .' Frank's pencil paused over his file.

The commanders politely accepted the information.

'Of course, news is coming in all the time. We'll keep you up to date.'

'Thank you.' General von Chemnitz nodded his burly head. 'We realize we are not up to date . . .'

'These are rapidly changing times, general. Who can hope to cope with so many events?'

'Indeed, so . . .' The red fat at the back of General von Chemnitz's neck trembled a little. 'And what will you be needing our forces to do?'

'Work with the boys, I should expect, general.' Frank laughed and glanced at all their faces. 'Seriously – we'll be needing your men to clean up any pockets of subversive activity after our first wave has gone over your particular areas. The details of that are what we're here to discuss just as soon as General Cumberland gets here.'

'There's the question of looting,' General de Jong of the Netherlands raised his elegant pen.

'Reclamation of goods. We have two basic categories here, gentlemen. Perishable commodities and non-perishable commodities. Most perishable commodities may be used by the divisions that come across them. Non-perishable commodities should be stored safely until a committee of senior officers has conferred as to their use and distribution. We have had the leaflets prepared which tell you how to cope with that problem. There are also leaflets available on Sexual Intercourse By Force, Sexual Intercourse By Consent, Sexual Intercourse By Unnatural Methods, Sexual Intercourse Between Members Of The Same Sex, Sexual Intercourse With Animals, Sexual Intercourse With Minors, Sexual Intercourse With Enemies Or Those Likely To Be Potential Enemies Or Enemy Sympathizers, Sexual Intercourse While On Active Military Duty, Conditions Under Which The Use Of Torture May Become Necessary, Conditions Under Which The Orders Of A Commanding Officer May Be Disobeyed, Conditions Under Which Allies May Be Killed Or Confined, and so on and so forth. General Cumberland and his staff have thrashed all these matters out to save you time and trouble. General Cumberland wrote most of the leaflets himself, in fact. He is a man of immense energy and thrust. An inspiration.'

Field Marshal Fry glanced at his wizened wrist. 'Good Lord! Look at the time! I say, do you mind if I bow out on this one? I promised a fellow a game of golf in a quarter of an hour. You'll keep my staff up to date, I take it.'

'Of course, Field Marshal.'

Fry shook hands with some of the other generals, saluted and hurried off the scene. Two or three others got up and made their apologies.

'I'm sure we can leave it with you.' General Groente of Belgium lifted his belly over the edge of the table. 'The wife ...'

172

'The children ...' said the youthful Field Marshal Denoël of Switzerland.

'The car ...' said pale General Ingrid-Maria Stafstrom of Sweden.

'Well, I guess this is cosier anyway.' Frank's eyes hardened.

'But you are so capable of "running the show". It is a compliment.' General von Chemnitz clicked his heels. 'Ah, here is ...'

They stood up as General Cumberland came in. He wore light battle-dress, his tunic open all the way down and his shirt unbuttoned to show his chest and medallion. Dark combat goggles were pushed up over his cap and his light blue eyes were steady in his weather-beaten face. He looked younger than fifty and he did not seem at all anxious about his immense responsibilities. As he shook hands with the other commanders he shuddered every time his flesh touched theirs.

'Now, gentlemen.' He sat down at the head of the table. 'I hope Frank's filled you in on the basics, uh?'

'I think they're in the picture,' said Frank.

'Great. But I'd like to briefly reiterate the ideology behind all this again for you. See, we've been sent over here because we heard you needed some help with a few of your problems. And we didn't just say we'd help – we put our money where our mouths were.

'And we sent you the guys to help you out. Well, I guess you needed more guys, and you got 'em. You got 'em without even having to ask. And you're welcome. We know the trouble you have and that's what we're here to put a stop to. We know what the Israelis are up to and we think we can maybe give 'em something to think about – so they'll damn well *stop* what they're up to before they do something really foolish.

'We know that your armies, your intelligence outfits and your civilian communities are riddled through and through with fifth columnists – with traitors – and we're doing something about that, too. When action's called for – we're the guys to call.'

He put his teeth together and smiled. 'Let me just read you something I got from back home the other day.' From his tunic pocket he took a clipping which he carefully unfolded and spread before him on the table. Then he began to read in a quiet but declamatory tone:

'Let's start looking at the situation in which we and the rest of the free-world forces involved find ourselves. It is not complex, not obscure, not hard for anyone to understand.

'We are losing the war.

'So many of the people on our side are being killed that the rest of them are thinking about quitting.

'That definition of losing, incidentally, is not only my own. It was taught to me by Admiral Bull Halsey before I covered the battle for Iwo Jima, the first time I saw mortal combat. The actions in the Rhine Valley now are no less obscene or exalting or decisive than were those in the grey sands cradling Mount Suribachi twenty-five years ago.

'Even the hideous casualty totals are in the same magnitude, though they have taken days instead of years to inflict; the fighting in Europe between the forces of our side and those who would bury us has cost more than 100,000 lives. Of the dead, only several hundred have been Americans.

'Of those, seven were men beside whom I had walked or parachute jumped or river forded or shared a stint of guard duty on a sandbagged emplacement at some place whose name we could not pronounce till we got there.

'Almost all US casualties are from the small group of Americans serving in active combat. Most US uniformed personnel do not actively risk their lives. Out of every five or six sent overseas, only one is exposed to actual daily fighting while the others serve in supporting roles. So those three millions of our men now in Europe add only several thousand to the active European armed forces which, including militia, now total more than twelve million.

'Those few exposed Americans, though, have accomplished something by their sheer character that no other Americans have been able to do in more than a decade. They have forced a major enemy to change tactics as a response to what they are doing.

'This is in utter contrast to what happened to free-world forces in Hungary and Algeria and Cuba and Formosa and Laos, where our side did all the second-guessing and did not once win.

'The fighting in Europe marks the first time that our side

n the eyes of the enemy has been applying a system of force so effectively that the other side considers we must be halted at all costs lest we start winning the war.

'What we have been doing right, of course, is to provide some superb leadership to the tough European fighting man.

'I have watched the working of the practice during fourteen months in the field with nine different combatant forces. The enemy fear it so greatly that killing Americans now is their priority tactical objective.

'The erstwhile ranking target used to be any European community leader; in September, almost a thousand mayors and provincial representatives were assassinated or abducted.

'Somehow, this fact seems not to have become known to most Americans and they impatiently ask what defect of will in the European people prevents formation of a stable democratic government.

'The facts as I saw them in the region where most Europeans live, the suburbs and the countryside, were not mysterious at all; there just haven't been enough surviving politicians, thanks to enemy raiding and the attendant atrocities.

'But beginning this fall, enemy tacticians issued orders that were a little different from their previous ones. And shorter, too. *Get the Americans.*

'These orders are not being disobeyed. Out of forty-two American mentors attached to European combat units, who happened to be billeted in one headquarters in the heart of Bavaria's most strategic area, nineteen were killed or wounded in two months. I know: I too was quartered there then, and the count is my own, not that of any public information officer back in Bonn.

'By the grisly economy of war, this change in enemy targeting is the ultimate stamp of effectiveness on what we at home have been taught cynically and incorrectly to call the "advisor system" of military aid to Europe.

'Obviously, it is more than that. "Advisors" do not become prime enemy targets.

'I submit with great pride that these Americans are not only advising; they are not just fighting in self-defence: Without any trappings of command – indeed, without even a shadow of command authority – they are leading.

'They are leading foreign troops simply because that's the way the troops want it. Why? Because each of these men, in the European troops' opinion, is the best soldier around and hence the leader most likely to bring them through victorious. And to put it bluntly, bring them back alive.

'In short, though the US seems to have hidden its virtue, the details of the honourable course it has taken in Europe, the Europeans know and salute it when the chips are down.

'Why "honourable"? Consider our defence treaty; it pledges to supply Europe whatever she lacks to win over communism. When it developed that in fact military leadership was a prime lack, we began delivering just what we'd promised.

'Well, then, why is there still a question about the outcome? Why aren't we winning?

'In my judgement, simply because we haven't sent *enough* of this leadership.'

The general paused, looked up and spoke softly. 'Well, gentlemen – that's the kind of support you're getting from the folks back home where I come from. I'll skip most of the rest – but I'll read you the last bit:

'All of which puts the determination of tomorrow's history where I have every confidence it best belongs: squarely into the hands of the people of the United States.

'It is for each of us to decide what we want to do and to give the government we have elected freely some clear evidence of our will to win, lose or draw.

'After all, it is not that administrative abstraction we call a government that will bear the final bloody consequence if we choose badly.

'It is us and our sons and daughters.'

General Cumberland looked reverently at the clipping as he folded it carefully and when he glanced up his eyes were chips of blue steel.

'That's how we feel. You know you can rely on us. The only way to win a war is to fight it. The road ahead will not be smooth and offer easy travelling. But the road map we're using today is a heck of a lot better than it has been. In the words of Patrick Henry as he stood before the Richmond

Convention and delivered his famous address – "They tell us, sir, that we are weak; unable to cope with so formidable an adversary. But when shall we be stronger? Will it be the next week or the next year? Will it be when we are totally disarmed, and when a British guard shall be stationed in each house? Shall we gather strength by irresolution and inaction?" – of course we will not! The United States will accept a decent negotiated peace in Europe. But it will not go, umbrella in hand, like Neville Chamberlain, to the aggressor, and let him write the settlement on his own expansionist terms. There can be no complaint about US Marines being sent to Europe, except that they might have been sent sooner. For years the Europeans – with token resistance from the United States – have been trying to defend themselves against raids, murder by stealth, sabotage and subversion. The results have been a mounting loss of American and European lives – no progress at all in ridding the continent of the invaders. Now the Europeans and the US have taken to offensive strikes of their own ... hitting where it hurts! And that's the way it's going to be, gentlemen, until the last enemy is destroyed and Europe can settle down to building the continent she wants in the way she wants to, without fear of attack from without or within. There's a wave back there and it's coming in fast – and that wave is American strength, gentlemen. American strength, American manhood, American know-how, American guts; American money, American dynamism, American bullets, American guns, American tanks, American planes, American freedom, American efficiency ...'

Frank took notes and the European commander stared in faint surprise at the C-in-C. Those nearest the door were already leaving and the others were rising from their chairs.

'American love, American humour, American health, American beauty, American virility ...'

The last general quietly closed the door behind him and General Cumberland raised his head at the sound.

'Have they deserted us, Frank?'

'I think they got the picture, general. I think their confidence is won.'

'I hope so, Frank. I tried to raise their morale. It sometimes seems to be the hardest job. They're all fairies, of course. Decadence is a terrible thing to witness. But maybe if we improve their conditions – give them a chance ...'

'They'll pull through.'

'God willing, Frank.'

3. It's KLM's 50th Anniversary. We Thought You'd Like to Share a Few Happy Moments

When Frank came back Jerry was still looking at General Cumberland whose lips moved as he scribbled rapidly in a notebook.

Frank stood beside Jerry and watched for a while. Then he turned the general off.

'It's rotten for him, really.' Jerry was sympathetic.

'He takes it well. The responsibility.' Frank crossed to the window and peered in the direction of St James's Park. 'Sometimes it seems there'll never be an end to it, Jerry. Or a beginning, in one sense, I suppose. There's so much to do – and so little time.'

'True.'

'I hope you're not brooding on our differences any more. After all, if brothers can't fall out occasionally, who can?'

'It all depends, a bit, on your position, Frank.'

Frank shrugged and spread his thin hands. 'You know me, Jerry. It's easy for you.'

'It is easier. You've got the heat death to contend with. I've always granted you that, Frank.'

'After all, what is a memory?'

'Perhaps nothing more than a hologram.'

'Exactly. Remember that dream of mine when we were young? A hologram on every billboard. A billboard the length of every street. A grid of streets that covered the globe ...' Frank shrugged. 'But it didn't prove to be as simple as that, did it, Jerry?'

'That's the difference between you and me. Where's my machine?'

'It's a question of cycles, I suppose.'

'Or anarchic equilibrium.' Jerry rested his hand on his vibra-gun. 'Come along, Frank.'

'You'd never get out, Jerry. And you'd lose a lot of potential friends.'

179

'I don't need friends.'

'You don't need enemies, either. I only want to strike a bargain with you. It could make us both rich – and extremely powerful. You've got to look to the future, old man.'

'I'm not too happy about these artificial divisions, Frank. I want to look to it all at once. I don't like the way you and your allies slice up time.'

'Somebody's got to do the dirty work.'

Jerry drew his gun. Frank drew his gun.

Jerry sighed. 'There doesn't seem a lot of point. Couldn't you just tell me where the machine is?'

'You tell me what it is, then.'

'It's a simple diffusion device,' lied Jerry. 'A randomizer. Nothing complicated.'

'It replicates conditions in the Shifter, is that it?'

'That's it.'

'Well, it wouldn't suit me, Jerry. I've never had much sympathy for that sort of thing. You know me – live and let live – but it wouldn't ...'

Jerry raised his gun.

'Well, it wouldn't! Christ – there are much better ways of having fun.'

'Where's the machine?'

'Derry and Toms Famous Roof Garden.'

'Thanks,' said Jerry and waited until Frank had put his gun back. 'Let me know something I can do for you.' He holstered his own vibragun.

'Nothing at this stage,' Frank said, riding swiftly into the new situation. 'You haven't got much of a chance of getting to that machine or of getting out of London alive. But if you should manage both things, then it's quite likely I'll be in a difficult position and you'll owe me a favour, won't you?'

'You've mellowed, Frank.'

'I'm coming apart, Jerry. I'm desperate.'

'It seems to be doing you good.' Jerry grinned. 'You're more mature.'

Frank sniffed. 'Call it what you like. I call it caution. You have to look after yourself when you get into my condition.'

'Well, let's hope I make it to Derry and Toms.'

Frank glanced at his watch. 'You just might, if they don't get around to that sector right away. I'm off to Milton Keynes in a few minutes. That's our new base. The general thinks it's cleaner. No population, you see. They never had a chance to fill it.'

'Sure. Well, don't take any wooden nickels.'

'Not from you, Jerry.'

'I'll be off, then.'

Jerry opened the door and the swords clashed under his nose.

'Let him through,' said Frank in a peculiar voice.

Jerry closed the door and looked up and down the corridor. He frowned as he contemplated the rigid guards and then came to a decision.

It was just as well to be on the safe side, to give himself some sort of edge. Frank was so shitty.

'If you ask me,' he said quietly, 'he's not what he seems to be. He's all bits and fucking pieces.'

He trod the soft carpets. The sunlight poured through the big window at the far end of the corridor and through it Jerry could see the green and gold of the quiet autumn trees.

It looked a nice day for a picnic.

Cut Two

POLARIS NUCLEAR SUB!

How proud you will be as commander of your own POLARIS SUB – the most powerful weapon in the world! What hours of imaginative play and fun as you and your friends dive, surface, manoeuvre, watch the enemy through the periscope and fire your nuclear missiles and torpedoes! What thrills as you play at hunting sunken treasures in pirate waters and exploring the strange and mysterious bottom of the deep ocean floor.

HOURS AND HOURS OF ADVENTURE

Sturdily constructed ... Comes complete with easy assembly instructions. Costs only $6.98 for this giant of fun, adventure and science. (Because of the POLARIS SUB's giant size we must ask for 75c shipping charges.)

MONEY BACK GUARANTEE

Order today and we will rush your POLARIS NUCLEAR SUB to you. Use it for 10 full days. If you don't think it is the greatest ever – the best toy you ever had – just send it back for full purchase price refund.

Real Confessions ad

1. Scream and Die, European Commie Homos, in Yank 'Cleanse and Burn' Offensive

t wasn't far to Derry and Toms, but the napalm was coming on heavy as Jerry drove west to the sound of Ronald Boyle's recorded voice booming in even tones from loudspeakers mounted in every flying thing.

BURN OUT THE CANCER
BURN OUT THE CANCER
BURN OUT THE CANCER
BURN OUT THE CANCER
BURN OUT THE CANCER
BURN OUT THE CANCER

The day was grey; the sunlight blocked by the planes whose steady roar echoed through the city.

BURN OUT THE CANCER
BURN OUT THE CANCER
BURN OUT THE CANCER
BURN OUT THE CANCER
BURN OUT THE CANCER
BURN OUT THE CANCER
BURN OUT THE CANCER

The napalm sheets kept falling.

BURN OUT THE CANCER
BURN OUT THE CANCER
BURN OUT THE CANCER
BURN OUT THE CANCER
BURN OUT THE CANCER
BURN OUT THE CANCER
BURN OUT THE CANCER

Jerry waited impatiently at Knightsbridge for the lights to change. Several buildings, including the recently rebuilt barracks of the Royal Horse Guards, were beginning to burn.

BURN OUT THE CANCER
BURN OUT THE CANCER
BURN OUT THE CANCER
BURN OUT THE CANCER

BURN OUT THE CANCER
BURN OUT THE CANCER
BURN OUT THE CANCER

He decided to go through the park and turned right. As he did so the first B52s came in low, streaming clouds of defoliant and making a thick fog that reduced visibility to a few feet.

Jerry slowed down and switched to his own air supply, turned his most powerful lamps into the swirling white mist, and kept going. He could see just far enough ahead to avoid hitting any large obstacles. Derry and Toms was in Sector D-7 and this was Sector G-6. Depending on their sweep, he had a little time before they started on D-7.

He was, as ever, impressed by the efficiency of the strike. By tomorrow, London should be completely Triple A Clean. His brother, with his liking for systems and his knowledge of London, had probably had a lot to do with the planning.

As the mist thinned a little he looked up, recognizing the hazy silhouettes of a squadron of General Dynamics F-111As lumbering across the sky followed by McDonnell F-4B Phantom IIs, F-4C Phantom IIs, RF-4 Phantom IIs, F-101B Voodoos, F-101C Voodoos, Republic F-105 Thunderchiefs, Ling-Temco-Vought (Chance Vought) F-8U Crusaders, Convair F-106 Delta Darts, Lockheed F-104 Starfighters, Convair F-102 Delta Daggars, Northrop F-5A Freedom Fighters, Ling-Temco-Vought A-7A Corsair IIs, North American F-100 Super Sabres, North American FJ Furies, Douglas F-6A Skyrays, Grumman F-11A Tigers, McDonnell M-3B Demons, Northrop F-89 Scorpions, North American F-86D Sabres and very much behind the others, Republic F-84F Thunderstreaks doing their best to keep up.

The planes passed and the helicopters chattered by. As far as Jerry could make out they were all heading due north, which meant that Derry and Toms, if it had so far missed the strike, would probably be okay for a little while.

He took a bearing off the Albert Memorial and bumped over the dying grass until he splashed into the Round Pond by accident and had to operate the screws for an instant as he crossed the pond and at last got to The Broad Walk near the London Museum, drove down The Broad Walk and came out on to a Kensington Road that was red with reflected fire.

light, but seemed as yet undamaged, though clouds of sodium cacodylate mixed with free cacodylic acid, water and sodium chloride drifted in the streets.

Elsewhere Jerry recognized n-butyl ester, isobutyl ester, tri-isopropanolamine, salt picloram and other chemicals and he knew that the park had got everything – Orange, Purple, White and Blue.

'Better safe than sorry.' He pulled up outside Derry and Toms.

Business appeared to have fallen off badly in the last few hours, though it was relatively peaceful here. In the distance Jerry heard the sound of falling buildings, the scream of rockets, the boom of the bombs, the shouts of the dying.

A boy and a girl ran out of the smoke, hand in hand, as he entered the store; they were on fire, making for the drinking fountain on the corner of Kensington Church Street.

The fire would probably help cope with the plague.

There was nothing like the chance of a fresh start.

2. The Man Behind the Face that 350 Million TV Viewers Know as the Saint

Although the defoliants hadn't yet reached the roof garden, there was a strong chemical smell as Jerry used his vibragun to shake down the door of an emergency exit and emerge into the Tudor Garden.

He wondered at first if the machine batteries had started to leak. They had been manufactured hastily, for the machine had originally been intended only as a prototype. It was Jerry's fault that he had tried it out in the Shifter and had lost it in the ensuing confusion.

Jerry placed the odour at last. It was Dettol.

The disinfectant had been used to hide another smell which he now recognized as the smell of corruption. It would have been good for the garden, of course, if things had been left alone. He wondered who had been here recently.

Everything was tidy and there wasn't a trace of an old lady. Jerry noticed with disappointment that the ducks had flown.

He wandered across to the Spanish Garden, watching as the blue heaven gradually filled with black smoke, and climbed the wall to look at the burning city and the insane jets wheeling about the sky in their dance of death. Napalm fell. Rockets raced.

'Out of time, out of touch,' murmured Jerry. It was what his father had always taught him. He didn't often feel this complacent. 'Goodbye, America.'

'Europe,' said a voice with a thick Russian resonance, 'can become the ultimate possibility pool. You're slowing down, Comrade Cornelius.'

Jerry shifted his position on the wall and looked down at the little man standing among the flowering ferns and dwarf palms, tugging at his goatee. 'You've been taking speech training.'

The man looked embarrassed and removed his rimless glasses. 'I can't stay long.'

'Is my machine here?'

'That's what I came to tell you about, comrade. I didn't think it was safe. I gave it to a friend of yours to look after. She was here until recently.'

'Captain Hargreaves?'

'I didn't realize, until she put on her uniform, that she was with the defenders.'

'Do you know where she is?'

'Presumably with the rest of her comrades, wherever that may be.'

'You've never been able to do anything right, have you, you old softie.' Jerry jumped down from the wall. 'Ah, well. It was nice of you to tell me.'

'I'm sure everything will work out. Won't it?'

'Keep your fingers crossed, comrade.'

The little man extended his hand. 'Well, if I don't see you again.' He vanished.

Jerry yawned. He was getting behind on his sleep. He left the roof garden as the first wave of planes arrived in Sector D-7, leapt down the stairs as the building began to shake, and reached the street as spluttering napalm flooded through the store.

He drove down Kensington High Street as fast as he could. He hoped Koutrouboussis and the rest were okay. If they'd been able to get out they should be safe enough at the Sunnydale Reclamation Centre.

He didn't feel particularly disappointed. After all, things had gone very easily up to now.

He made for Milton Keynes.

Extraction

Jews get out of Palistine it's not your home anyway! Moses
was the first traitor and Hitler was the Messiah!!!
                                    Black militant placard, Harlem

1. Outlaw in the Sky

Jerry left the burning city behind and headed up the M1. It was a wide, lonely road, through the hushed countryside.

He turned on the radio and tuned it to Radio Potemkin. It was playing the Yardbirds. The Moquettes, The Zephyrs, Mickie Most, The Downliners Sect, Rey Anton and the Peppermint Men, The Syndicats, The Cheynes, The Cherokees, Cliff Bennett and The Rebel Rousers. Unable to bear either the nostalgia or the quality, Jerry switched over to Radio John Paul Jones which was in the middle of putting over *The Vibrating Ether Proves The Cosmic Vortex*, the latest hit by Orniroffa, the Nip Nightingale. All art, thought Jerry, aspired to the condition of Muzak. What would William Morris have thought?

It was at times like this that the brain needed balming. He turned to his taper and selected Schoenberg's Quartet No. 2, left the M1 and took a winding lane towards Oxford.

Soon he could see the white shell of the city shining in the distance. The concrete roof was good for anything except the H-Bomb.

He slowed down as he reached the opening of the tunnel and drove through to emerge in the shadowy darkness of Magdalen Bridge.

The dim light from the central lamp at the highest part of the roof was reflected by the spires of the city. Power was failing, but Oxford survived.

Jerry felt the cold. The High was full of a strange sticky dampness and black-coated figures crept miserably along beside the walls, while every so often hollow, echoing shouts and clatterings broke the stillness. The hissing noise of his own car seemed menacing.

Stopping the Phantom VI in the car park of the Randolph Hotel he walked to the Ashmolean Museum, pushed open the heavy wooden doors and paused. A few candles in brackets on the walls lit a sinister avenue of Tompion and Knibb longcase clocks which had all stopped at a quarter past twelve. He began to walk.

The sound of his footsteps was like that of a huge pendulum, regular and ponderous. He came to the locked door at the end of the avenue and took a key from his pocket, turned it in the lock, opened the door and descended the stone staircase, lighting his way with his torch.

Climbing downwards for half-an-hour he at last reached a tunnel which led to another door. Unlocking this, he came to a room containing a small power plant. He crossed to the plant and depressed a lever.

The plant whispered and then hummed softly and steadily. Lights went on. Jerry switched off his torch, passed through two more empty chambers until he came to a fourth room which was lined on three sides with cupboards that had mirrors set into their panels. The cupboards had been imported from Sweden nine years earlier. The mirrors were more recent.

The room was carpeted with a deep, red, Russian rug. On it stood a couch draped with white mink covers and yellow silk sheets. It was unmade. Against the wall near the door was a neat console operating a series of small monitor screens and microtronic indicator boards, all slightly archaic in design and function but still in good working order. Jerry had not been here since he had left the seminary.

Sitting on the couch, he tugged off his block-heeled boots; he removed his jacket and his shoulder holster and dropped them on the floor, pulled back the pillows and touched a stud on the control panel set in the low headboard. The console activated, he lay and watched it for a bit until he felt up to visiting the morgue.

The room had become unfamiliar, yet a lot of things had happened here. The Shifter gateways had been erected, the earliest prototype of the machine had been built, the Web completed and, of course, those ridiculous books had been written. It had been a rapid development really, from priest to politician to physicist, but it had been necessary and, he supposed, inevitable.

He was drained. He smiled and shrugged. Perhaps he had better visit the Web before he went to the morgue. It was still very cold in the room. It would take a while for the place to warm up.

This had been his grandfather's complex originally, before the old man had moved to Normandy, and his father had inherited it, passing it on to him. His father had built and stocked the morgue, too.

He got up shivering, opened one of the mirrored panels and stepped through into a well-lit corridor with four steel doors on each side and another steel door at the end. He rested his palm against the fourth door on the right and it opened. A peg behind the door supported a clean black car coat. Jerry put it on and buttoned up. The schizophrenia had been bad at first, his father had said. He had been lucky not to inherit the worst of it.

There were ten drawers set low into the far wall. Each drawer was labelled with a name. Jerry opened the first drawer on the left and looked down into the eyes of the pale, beautiful girl with the tangled black hair.

He touched the cold skin of her breasts.

'Catherine ...'

He stroked the face and drew a deep breath.

Then he bent down and picked her up, carrying her from the morgue and back to the bed chamber with the console.

Placing her in the bed, he stripped off the rest of his clothes and lay beside her, feeling the heat flow out of his body into hers.

His life was so dissipated, he thought. But there was no other way to spend it.

'Catherine ...'

She stirred.

He knew there could only be a few seconds left.

'Catherine.'

The eyes opened and the lips moved. 'Frank?'

'Jerry.'

'Jerry?' Her perfect brow frowned slightly.

'I've got a message for you. There's some hope. That's the message. There's a chance of love. Mum ...'

Her eyes warmed, then faded, then closed.

Trembling with a terrible cold, Jerry began to cry. He staggered from the bed, fell to his knees, got up and lurched from the chamber into the corridor, pressing his frozen palm against the first door on his left.

The door opened stiffly, almost reluctantly.

Jerry leaned against it as it closed, peering through his blurred eyes at the rustling machine before him.

Then he flung himself at the singing red, gold and silver webs and gasped and grinned as they enmeshed him.

Why was resurrection so easy for some and so difficult for others?

2. Beyond the X Ecliptic

When he had filed Catherine again, Jerry whistled a complicated piece of Bartok and returned, radiant and replete, to his cosy room to look at himself in the mirrors.

Time to be moving; moves to be timing.

He opened a cupboard and regarded his wardrobe. The clothes were somewhat theatrical and old-fashioned but he had no choice. His nearest wardrobe to Oxford was now in Birmingham, the only major city in the area which had not needed cleaning, and he had never fancied Birmingham much at the best of times.

He selected a military-style green jacket, a suède shako with a strap that buttoned under his chin, matching suède britches, green jackboots and a shiny green Sam Browne belt with a button-down holster for his vibragun. A short green pvc cape secured by a silver chain over one shoulder, and the ensemble was complete.

He left the little complex and closed the door behind him.

Shining the torch up the stone staircase he climbed to the top and opened the surface door. Then, stopping at each and winding them up, he walked back down the avenue of long-case clocks. The gallery was soon filled with their merry ticking.

As he strolled away from the Ashmolean towards the car-park of the Randolph Hotel, he heard the clocks begin to strike nine o'clock.

He started the Phantom VI and turned the car into the Broad, switched the taper to Nina Simone singing *Black Swan*, and lay well back in the driving seat until he reached the Western airlock which he passed through without difficulty. He blinked as he broke into the bright, warm morning.

Soon he could see Milton Keynes.

The new conurbation rose out of the greenish ground mist, each great tower block a different pastel shade of pale chrome yellow, purple, gamboge, yellow ochre, chrome orange, vermilion, scarlet, red (ost), crimson, burnt sienna, light red, cobalt, cerulean blue, turquoise, ultramarine, prussian blue, mauve, leaf green, emerald, sap green, viridian, hookers green, burnt umber, vandyke brown, orange (ost), ivory black and grey (ost).

Entering the quiet streets of the great village, with its trim grass verges and shady trees, Jerry was filled with a sense of peace that he rarely experienced in rural settlements. Perhaps the size of the empty buildings helped, for most of them were over eighty feet high, arranged around a series of pleasant squares with central fountains splashing a variety of coloured, sparkling water or with free form sculptures set in flower gardens. There were terraced gardens with vines and creepers on the buildings themselves and the air was full of butterflies, mainly red admirals and cabbage whites.

Jerry drove at a leisurely pace until he came to the middle of the conurbation. Here were the main administration buildings and shopping arcades, the schools and the play areas, and here were parked the armoured vehicles, the tanks and the helicopters of the advisory force. Neat newly painted signs had been put up and it was easy for Jerry to park his car and make for General Cumberland's headquarters in the tall, domed building that the planners had intended for the town hall and which now flew the Stars and Stripes.

As Jerry climbed the steps, a detachment of unhappy marines broke from the building and surrounded him with a ring of sub-machine-guns. 'I was hoping I'd find Frank Cornelius here,' Jerry said mildly.

'What you want with Colonel Cornelius, boy?'

'I have some information for him.' A faint shock ran from the left hemisphere to the right of Jerry's brain.

'What sort of information, fella?'

'It's rather secret.'

The marines sniffed and rubbed their noses with their forearms, keeping their steely eyes fixed on him.

'You'd better tell the colonel I'm here, I think.'

'What's your name?'

'He'll know who it is if you describe me.'

One of the marines broke away and trotted inside. The circle closed up. Jerry lit a Romeo y Julieta and dropped the aluminium tube on the ground. Still staring unblinkingly at his

194

prisoner's face, a marine with pursed lips kicked the tube violently away.

Frank hurried out.

'Jerry! You made it! Great!'

The marines withdrew behind Jerry and came to the salute with a crash of boots and armour.

'Did you have any luck with the machine?' Frank put a cold arm round Jerry's shoulder and guided him into the new town hall.

'I can't complain.' Jerry spoke through his cigar. 'And are you satisfied?'

'*Relatively*, Jerry. Look, we'll go to my private quarters. That's the best idea, eh?'

They went through a glass door, crossed the open quadrangle and entered the building's northern wing. 'It's just here.' Frank stopped, unlocked his door and led Jerry into an airy, pleasant room in which Rose Barrie was arranging flowers on a sideboard.

'That's fine, Rose, thanks,' Frank smiled. The girl left.

'You're pretty loathsome, Frank.' Jerry took a golden chrysanthemum from the vase and smelled it.

'So would you be. I was never the favoured son, Jerry. I had to fight for what I wanted. You had it easy.'

'Until you fought for what you wanted.'

'Oh, that ...'

'I've just been to see Catherine.'

'How is she? I was wilder in those days, Jerry.'

'She's keeping pretty well.'

'Our family always were great survivors.' Frank grinned. 'Do you want a ... ? No, I suppose not. But let's face it, Jerry. You got where you were by luck – by intuition, if you like. I had to do everything by thinking. Hard thinking. Logical thinking.'

'It made you tense, Frank.'

'That's the price you pay.'

Jerry put the chrysanth back. Then he smashed the vase from the sideboard and looked at the fallen flowers, the spilled water and the broken glass on the carpet.

'Don't lose your temper, Jerry.' Frank was laughing. 'You are a hothead! What's wrong, old sweat?'

'I'd love to be able to kill you, Frank. Kill you, Frank. Kill you, Frank.'

Frank spread the fingers at the end of his extended right arm. 'Jesus, Jerry, so would I ...'

'I'd love to be able to kill you, Frank.'

'That's a remote possibility.'

'It's all too fucking remote.'

Jerry swayed from the waist, eager for his gun.

'Calm down, Jerry, for Christ's sake.' Frank snapped his fingers at his sides. 'You'll need removing. Is this the time? Is this the place?'

'Space is all you ever fucking think about.'

'Somebody has to. Listen, Jerry, I've got a moral responsibility. I never had that. I *have* changed. I could lose it all. Split. I'm going to keep it. The power's building up.'

'You'd have thought Einstein had never happened!'

'Maybe he shouldn't have happened. It's running too wild. We need something concrete – definite – solid. Something hard. Authoritative ...'

'I want something easy.'

'Exactly. Connect, Jerry – just for a moment.'

'Shit ...'

'Technology is potential freedom from brutality. I should know. The old can't riot and have no power. We must forfeit the right to breed in order to retain the right to breathe. Immortality is just around the corner!'

'Mortality is *space*.'

'You've too much imagination. That's what I mean.'

'What's the matter with you, Frank? You ...'

'I'm older. You can never be that.'

'Piss ...'

'Man is the only animal with the imaginative characteristic developed to any degree. No competition, see? The trait has become *over-developed*. A survival characteristic turned into an anti-survival characteristic. We must limit imagination. Destroy it, if necessary, in the majority, limit it in the rest. Jerry, it's our only chance to get back to something worthwhile. To normality.'

Jerry stared vaguely at his brother. 'Get back? Get back? But we're moving on. The abstract ...'

'. . .can only destroy civilization . . .
. . . as we know it.'

'You see.'

'See? Death.'

'Death – and life.'

'Sure.'

'Then . . . ?'

'Kill you, Frank.'

'No!'

Jerry felt faint. 'You're fouling things up, Frank. You were nicer when you knew it. Mom always said in time . . .'

'Forget Time.' Frank slapped the sideboard. 'That's what's important right now. A cleaning up. A getting back to fundamentals.'

'Forget Space.'

'Jerry – when I returned there had to be some constructive action. We mustn't fight.'

'Catherine. You killed our sister.'

'You killed her.'

'You made me.'

'Who's the guilty one?'

'Guilt? There you go again.' Jerry relaxed. 'Well, I suppose you just saved your life. Boredom is a great preserver.' He stretched. 'So you've decided to think ahead? I can't see it myself.'

'You won't give yourself a chance. You won't give me a chance.'

Jerry began to pick up the pieces of broken glass and put them on the sideboard. He gathered the flowers into a bunch and crossed the room to a mock Tudor table which had an empty vase on it. He put the flowers in the vase. 'It's a question of identity, Frank. What the hell. A wild environment, an integrated identity.'

'We're clearing things up. Tidying the world.'

'You might just as well be in the political age. You can't bring it back, Frank.'

'We will.'

'Not for long.'

'You'll see.'

'But you know what I'm out to do, don't you?'

'Randomize. The equilibrium of anarchy.'

'More or less.'

'You won't succeed. History's against you, Jerry.'

'That's the difference between you and me, Frank. I'm against History.'

'Where are you going?'

Jerry made for the door. 'I've got to look up an old flame. You don't mind me hanging around for a while, do you?'

'I'd rather you did. Have you got the machine with you?'

'No.'

'Then I'd rather you did.'

'I'll be seeing you soon, Frank.'

'Bet on it.'

3. The Prison of the Stars

Jerry found Flora Hargreaves by the fountain, behind the M-60 tanks.

'You're just as I remember you,' he said.

She smiled, smoothing her olive uniform. 'You never told...'

'No.'

'Thanks.'

'You met a friend of mine in London, didn't you? He gave you something to look after.'

'That's right, Jerry.'

'I need it now.'

'You do? You'd better come back to my place. I've got nice quarters. There's plenty of space for everybody.'

They walked between the tanks and crossed the square to the violet building opposite the town hall. All around the square the marines were relaxing, chatting to the WACs, smoking, sipping soft drinks, cleaning their Navy Colts.

'It's been pretty tough for them,' said Flora. 'But I guess they know how to take it.'

'They can take anything by the look of them.'

'Almost anything.' Flora straightened her shoulders. She winked at him. 'It's gotten to be a rotten war, Jerry. I sometimes wonder what you people make of it. It can be hard, sometimes, to take the overall view when your own country's ... well ...'

Jerry sucked in his breath. 'It has to be this way. Maybe if the CIA were still around things would be better.'

'I guess.'

'They've nothing against – you know – consorting?'

'If you're here, Jerry, you've had security clearance. That's all they want to know. It's my leave. I can do what I like.'

They entered the building and climbed the concrete stairs to the first floor, walking along a cool, shady corridor until they came to her room. She turned the handle and threw the door open with a sweeping gesture. *'Après vous!'*

Jerry padded in and eyed the room. It was very feminine. There were a lot of soft toys on the bed, posters of British beauty spots on the walls, a helmet and battle overalls hanging over a chair, a .22 in a holster on a stack of Penguin paperbacks, a neat kitchenette through an archway. The room was sunny. Flora drew the blinds.

'The machine,' said Jerry.

She went to her wardrobe. There were three print dresses in it. She bent and Jerry looked at her thighs. She straightened, holding something black, square and heavy, and Jerry looked at her eyes. She widened them. 'Is this it?'

'This is it.' Jerry laughed with relief. 'Put it down. Aha!'

As she put it on the floor he seized her, running his hand up her leg and down her regulation drawers; kissing her wide, soft, hot, damp, lively mouth; running his other hand through her sweet auburn hair; guiding her to the bed and fucking her with enormous joy and energy.

'Well, that was nice,' she said. 'I always knew . . .'

'Come off it.' He gave her one of her Kents and lit another for himself.

'Is the box valuable?'

'It means the world to me.'

'It just looks like some sort of geiger counter – something like that.'

'It's a bit more versatile.'

'Tell me what it is, Jerry.' She curled a leg over his leg and licked his left nipple.

'There's no real word for it. Nothing – *authentic*. One of its functions is as a sort of randomizer. It can produce all the alternatives at once. There's a lot of power in that little box.'

'A computer? Multivalue logic?'

'Not a computer. Far from it. Almost the opposite, in one sense. It breaks down the barriers. It lets the multiverse – well – "in".'

'That isn't a proper word.'

'It's everything.'

'What's everything?'

'You're everything, Flora. But now you can be mirrored by your environment. It creates a human environment for a human being. It can also speed up various basic processes.'

'That's an explanation?'

'Explanations shouldn't be necessary between us, Flora.'

There was a cool breeze and a neigh.

Frank stood in the open door, his upper lip curled like a mule's, his needle-gun in his hand. He came in and closed the door, crossing to the black box. 'I thought so.'

'You're so fucking high-minded.' Jerry climbed over Flora and sat on the edge of the bed, pulling on his underpants and socks. 'You can't destroy that machine without risking the whole bloody universe going wild.'

'Isn't that what you want?'

'Moderation in all things, Frank. That's anarchy.'

'You're a traitor, Captain Hargreaves. Consider yourself under arrest.'

Flora shrugged and pushed the bedclothes back with her feet.

Jerry crossed to the chair and picked up his shirt, pulling it over his head. 'Well, Frank, I think a certain equilibrium's been achieved, don't you?'

'You can talk of equilibrium with this –' Frank kicked at the black box – 'in existence. This chaos machine.'

'Oh, come now, Frank. We're not even sure if it has an

entropic effect or not. It's an experimental model. That's how I came to lose it in the first place – I created the field and then couldn't find the machine in it.' Jerry laughed. 'Ironic, eh? I've got to test it. Find out exactly what it does do.'

'At the expense of society.'

'Well, that's how you see it.'

Jerry put on his other clothes and buckled his Sam Browne belt. 'That's better. You're always catching me with my pants down.'

'It used to be nice. But you know what happened the last time. What has this machine to do with Catherine?'

'Work it out. It's the creation of all possible worlds. It can channel energy – re-divert it – re-form it ... it is hope.'

'Bloody romantic,' said Frank.

'Who's Catherine?' said Flora.

'My aunt ...'

'Our sister,' said Frank.

'Have it your way.' Jerry licked his lips. 'Still, this has nothing much to do with the current situation.'

'What is your relationship?' Flora frowned.

'It's become a little ambiguous of late,' Jerry told her. Frank had swung the needle-gun into line with his heart. 'I suppose it boils down to a matter of identification, in the long run.'

'Identity!'

Frank snarled and squeezed the trigger as Jerry dropped behind the chair and drew his vibragun.

'If either of us hits that machine,' said Jerry, 'we might find out a lot about identity.'

Frank hesitated then lowered his gun. 'All right, Jerry. Let's talk like rational men.'

'I'm not sure how it's done.'

Flora Hargreaves rose suddenly and threw the bedclothes over Frank's head. Jerry jumped out and thumped his relative on the back of his neck with the barrel of the vibragun. He fell down heavily. Jerry took the needle-gun out of the tangle of sheets and handed it to Flora. 'He couldn't bear it if you shot him.'

'Why?'

'Oh, well. It's all a matter of ritual, you see.' Jerry uncovered Frank whose face had aged. He began to shiver, rubbing nervously at his arms, passing his hands over his head. 'He lives by precedent.'

'I'm losing heat, Jerry. I'm losing heat, Jerry. I'm losing heat, Jerry.'

'And dynamic, I suppose.' Jerry pushed Frank's chest with his vibragun. 'Move along there, Frank. Can you manage the box, Flora?'

'I'll have to get some clothes on first. And pack.'

'Wear your uniform. Pack your dresses. Okay?'

'Okay.'

Flora quickly got ready and lifted the heavy box. Jerry pushed the cringing Frank forward. 'We'll make for my convertible. We'll take you along with us, Frank. This environment isn't doing you any good at all.'

They descended the stairs, then descended the steps that led them into the square. Marines still stood about in the sun, taking a well-deserved rest from the dirty business of war. Jerry hid his vibragun with his cloak and the three of them walked slowly to the car. Flora got in the back with the box. Frank sat beside Jerry as he started the Phantom VI up.

'Where are we going?' Flora asked.

'Our first duty is to get Frank into a rest home. It's not far from here. A couple of hours' drive. I think he'll last until then.'

Flora sniffed. 'You think so?'

'He is beginning to niff a bit, I must admit.'

Saturation

Female Auto-Erotic Practices

Out of print for years. By Havelock Ellis, M.D., world's most famous sexologist. New illustrated edition.

Subjects include: initiation; auto-erotic practices with males; masturbation as the cause and cure of frustrations in marriage, various technic employed (both clitoral and vaginal); objects used for vaginal and urethral masturbation.

The use of artificial penes; mutual masturbation (both homosexual and heterosexual); psychological factors; fantasies, erotic dreams; incestuous masturbation (between brother/sister, uncle/niece, father/daughter as well as a case of initiation involving mother and son).

Auto-eroticism among dis-satisfied wives, girlhood experiments (with both sexes); initiations of boys by older women, nurses, etc.; club contests; public masturbation; breast stimulation; modern concepts of masturbation; primitive concepts; etc.

Illustrations include: artificial penes (both single-ended and double-ended for lesbian activities); other masturbatory devices; auto-erotic humour; auto-erotic symbols; childhood postures as well as women depicted in various auto-erotic attitudes. $3.00.

1. Bizarre Fatherhood Trap Exposed!

When Jerry, Flora and Frank arrived at Sunnydale Reclamation Centre, Matron greeted them with some eagerness.

'You've done the place up nicely.' Jerry gave the rebuilt centre the once-over as they stood in the drive by the car.

'What with all the emergency cases coming in during recent months, Mr Cornelius, we had to work quickly. Och, we've been that understaffed! Working with no proper instructions from administration ... There's no much left of your wee mansion o'course.'

'We have to cannibalize where necessary.' Jerry glanced sadly at Flora and past her to where he saw the shell of his little Dutch mansion.

'It's a shame,' said Flora.

'And what's yon wee chappy so upset aboot?' Matron looked professionally at the crumpled figure of Frank who sat in the front seat covering his face with his thin hands and mewling to himself.

'Another emergency, I'm afraid, Matron. A special case ...'

'Aye. That's what they all say.'

'Could you put him in a blank tank right away?'

'Is it wise, Mr Cornelius?'

'It's urgent.'

'A rather crude ...'

'Don't worry. He's a rather crude patient.'

'If you say so, sir. I'll get a couple of the lads tae take him in.' Matron went back through the main door and re-emerged with two assistants who picked Frank up and bore him, tightly foetal now, off.

Koutrouboussis, in an elegant blue mohair lounge suit with matching shirt and tie, his face and hands bandaged, came out of the door after Matron had gone in. He glanced sourly at Jerry. 'Having fun?'

'Can't complain. You appear to have left London in a hurry. How are Maureen and Barbara?'

'They were bubbled up,' Koutrouboussis said thoughtfully.

'Ah. This is Captain Hargreaves. Captain Hargreaves, this is Mr Koutrouboussis. He's a member of my organization.'

'You run an organization?' Flora raised her eyebrows.

'Six of one, half a dozen of the other.'

'How do you do?' Koutrouboussis gave a tiny, stiff bow, winced with pain and seemed to have difficulty turning his eyes on Jerry again. 'Did you get the machine?'

'Flora had it. It's in the back of the car.'

'So we can begin work. About bloody time. I'm sick to death of my particular role. I need a break.'

'We could all benefit from a change.'

'Can we get down to the lab now?'

'You can if you like. I'm a bit anxious about the inner man.' Jerry looked enquiringly at Flora. 'Could you do with a bite?'

She laughed. 'You know I could!'

Jerry escorted her into the cool, sweet-smelling interior of the reclamation centre.

2. Doctors Prove Sex Guilts Make You Impotent!

Jerry walked between the rows of blank tanks in the long, hushed ward.

Each tank had its indicators, its curled, black figure, its tube running from the head to the surface to the connections along the edges. He studied the coded plates on the base of each tank and eventually found Frank. He was hanging in the exact centre of his tank. Nothing moved. Every dial registered zero.

Jerry turned to the engineer who walked slowly down the other side of the aisle checking readings against sheets on a clipboard.

'Number 30005. Any anticipation yet, Alvarez?'

The engineer shrugged.

'Too early.'

Jerry licked his lower lip.

'Fair enough.'

3. The Nympho Cossack Queen of the Bloody Steppes

Catherine, in all her sweetness, stared at him through the darkness of the room and he sat up in the bed, his hand clawing into Flora's right breast so that she screamed and Catherine disappeared and Jerry slapped her mouth and punched her stomach and shrieked and ran from the room, and staggered through the galleries until he came back to the blank tank ward and reached Frank and smashed at the glass with his fists so his hands streamed with blood and the fluid from the tank bathed them.

Frank sank.

4. I Trained the Nude Girl Boxers of Bangkok

Naked, Jerry went back to the bedroom and gathered up his gun while Flora wept.

'It's not your fault,' he said. 'But it's terror time, I'm afraid.'

The cynics had got through. He was possessed.

5. Swamp Lust!

Jerry crossed to the lab wing, holding his gun tight against his thigh. There were lights. He opened the door. Koutrouboussis looked up red-eyed.

'You may be black,' he said, 'but you look juicy to me.'

'Any results?' asked Jerry.

'We needed you. You were fucking about.'

'Well, I'm not fucking about now.' Jerry tied his gun by its trigger guard to a lock of his hair so that the weapon rested against his neck.

The black box stood on the bench. A score of fine leads ran from it and were connected to other instruments. Jerry pulled them out.

'You won't need those. It's to do with instinct, you see.' He flexed his fingers.

'There's more than one way of skinning a cat,' said Koutrouboussis mildly.

6. Just Found: $10,000,000 in Pirate Treasure! Millions Still Untouched!

'That ought to do it.' Jerry straightened up and closed the lid of the box. 'Ready to go, Mr Koutrouboussis.'

'Glad to hear it.'

There was a wet sound behind them. Flora Hargreaves supported a bleary Frank who had his needle-gun in his hand.

'You look nice in rubber,' Jerry said, 'but it's all that's holding you together.'

Frank groaned. 'I've a moral duty to perform, you filth.'

Jerry tilted his head so that his gun swung on to his shoulder. Frank steadied his hand.

'Why are you involving yourself in this, Flora?' Jerry folded his arms across his chest.

'I give back what I get, you bastard.'

'Then you'd better give me Frank.' Jerry laughed. 'You know very well what will happen if you hit the box, Frank.'

'Well – Jerry – I don't – have to – take the – risk ...' Frank drooled.

'I suppose not.'

'You're the only – one – who knows which – button – to press ...'

'Well. Mr Koutrouboussis ...'

Koutrouboussis screamed as Frank's gun moved and the needle hit him in the knee.

'Good,' said Frank thickly. 'It's ...' He squeezed the trigger again but Jerry was sliding across the floor and taking cover behind a rustling hallucimat, untangling the vibragun from his hair and brushing the cobwebs from his nose just as the door opened again and Bishop Beesley and Mitzi, closely followed by a man wearing the red robes of a Roman Catholic cardinal, entered the room. They all wore crossed bandoliers of bullets and carried Italian Mausers. Mitzi took Frank's needle-gun away from him and darted a disgusted look at Flora who was

211

nursing her injured breast.

'By the way, Mr Cornelius,' said Bishop Beesley as he frisked Frank for pleasure. 'You'll be happy to know we've taken Karen into the fold again, poor thing.'

'How is she?'

Beesley shook his head. 'She's not the woman you remember, I'm afraid. Is that the box? Would you mind, cardinal?'

The cardinal hung his gun over his shoulder and lifted the box in his arms.

Mitzi glanced at Flora, then at Jerry, and with a gesture of compassion plugged Frank in the heart. Frank slapped down on the floor.

'Just a minute!' Jerry was offended. 'That was my bloody brother!'

'He was going to kill you, Herr Cornelius.'

Jerry stayed behind the hallucimat, his vibragun raised. 'You'd better put that box down, cardinal. I know religion wants to survive, but ...'

The cardinal turned his swarthy, questioning features in Bishop Beesley's direction.

'Oh, Mr Cornelius knows his weapon would seriously upset his machine's mechanism.' Beesley lowered his rifle. 'It's not our intention to destroy either you or your invention, Mr Cornelius, as you well know. We intend to save both – for everybody's benefit. We have a great deal of work to undo yet, haven't we?'

Jerry sighed.

'I've got a good mind to ...'

'Of course you have. You're so impulsive.'

'You couldn't operate it. It needs love, not – power.'

'Perhaps.'

'Oh, take the fucker. I haven't got anything left.'

Mitzi looked at the needle-gun. Then she frowned at Flora and, by way of an experiment, stitched a line of slivers across Flora's throat.

As the blood sprang out, Flora put her hand up, then let it fall again, then toppled backwards. Mitzi laughed and shot Koutrouboussis while she was at it.

212

'Do you believe in premonitions?' Jerry asked as they left. 'Or devils?'

'It depends on the source, Mr Cornelius.' Bishop Beesley rummaged in his pocket and found a large piece of walnut fudge. 'We'll be seeing you soon, I hope.'

4. FINAL
OPERATION

Guilt and fear are amongst the most soul-destroying, fatal and disintegrating emotions and experiences that come to man. Guilt because of wrong doing, unconfessed, unrepented of, and uncleansed causes havoc and must be got rid of by Jesus alone. Psychiatrists have their couches to handle this, but they are helpless for only Jesus can meet this need. Did you know that it has now been revealed that there are more psychiatrists that commit suicide than any other profession, so it is obvious they do not have the answer. Jesus, alone, upon full, whole-hearted, and honest confession, is able to deal with a guilt complex and cleanse and deliver utterly.

Len J. Jones, *The Evidence*, December 1967

Radiation Treatment

End result: CANCER OF THE CERVIX

The March issue of *McCalls* reports that 'Cancer of the cervix seems to be linked with the early loss of virginity and promiscuity on the part of young girls, according to three recent reports ... patients with cervical cancer ... had a greater number of sexual partners than comparable women who did not develop cancer ... Monogamy in sex appeared to reduce the risk of cancer.'

Newsweek (October 21, 1968) reports that: 'Researchers have long suspected that cancer of the cervix, which afflicts some 40,000 women per year, is a venereal disease ... most common among promiscuous women.'

... 'Enlightened modernists' cry for more sexual freedoms to undo the repressive sexual inhibitions of society and make people better off. How could these self impressed, lawless intellectuals explain the fact that the large majority of students who need psychiatric help *have already experienced this sexual freedom?*

They simply IGNORE these facts. They rant about sexual permissiveness and sexual looseness. Proof? They don't need it. Satisfy the animal lusts of the people and they will all flock to your side.

The PLAIN TRUTH, January 1969

1. Come Away Melinda

Jerry didn't mind the bombs as much as the rock scene. He wouldn't care what they sent so long as it wasn't Simon and Garfunkel.

It was like something out of 1962.

He switched off the radio.

Time to turn the lamp on bright.

'Una!'

2. That's No Way to Say Goodbye

A killing scene from now on. You couldn't stay smooth forever. Love seemed to have died.

He began to assemble his gun again, ignoring Matron's panicky knock on the door.

He picked a scarlet shirt with a huge rolled button down collar and frilly cuffs, scarlet velvet bell-bottoms, crimson suède boots, vermilion frock coat, scarlet cord cap. He combed his milk-white hair and crooned a tune to himself, clipped on his yellow chamois shoulder holster and stepped out into the soft night and his smooth car.

As he drove, he considered the stars. It would all be over in a flash.

'Mother.'

3. Sisters of Mercy

Somewhere a clock had stopped.

Jerry checked his watches.

They were running slow, but they were running.

He checked the car clock. It ticked painfully on.

Overwhelmed by a sense of urgency Jerry took the car up to a hundred and fifty. As it flew towards the dawn, he sighted Oxford's dreaming dome.

The day brightened. The sun appeared. Jerry glared at it with tears in his eyes. His heart beat rapidly, but he was filled with a growing stillness.

Was it too late?

Was Beesley's shit hitting the fan?

He roared into the concrete cavern and drove past the gloomy spires, squealing to a stop outside the Ashmolean, charging through its doors and running down the dark avenue of slurring longcase clocks.

'Catherine!'

4. Love Me Do

The morgue was colder than ever.

He opened the drawer and saw that a thin veil of ice had formed over Catherine's body.

He pressed his hands to her breasts and forced his heat into her.

This time she did not stir, but the ice gradually evaporated, then reformed on his body. Feebly he brushed at it, leaned on the drawer until it was closed, stumbled from the morgue to the room where the red, gold and silver machine took him into its webs.

The machine's voice was faint, its rustling sluggish, and it was a very long time before Jerry revived enough to hear the clock within him begin to move again.

Jerry Cornelius ran across the hall and into another steel room that contained nothing but a huge tape deck. He activated the deck and the twenty-inch spools slowly started to revolve.

He twisted the volume control up to full; give it maximum bass and treble response.

The Deep Fix began to play *That's My Baby*. The old strobes went bravely at it. The wall drifted apart.

Jerry entered the Shifter, nervous as a cat.

'Love?'

5. It's Hard to be a Saint in the City

Sweet Orb Mace appeared for a moment. She looked sad. Jerry dashed through the Shifter.

Scenes took a long time and a long time to go.

The jewelled air was pretty dull breathing.

Jerry saw himself sixteen times – black, white, male, female – and he was dead.

He raced across the flat, grey, infinite plain, his gun in his hand, sniffing the frigid wind.

There was no doubt that Beesley was operating the machine, had somehow managed to put it into reverse. Though it would mean the same thing in the end, Ragnarok Day was being put back and it didn't suit him. It had to be this Cycle or nothing.

He wheeled and the air was cold brass.

Bishop Beesley stood beside a contraption. At its centre were the belching boiler and the frantically moving pistons and cogs of an ancient red and black steam engine. A system of clockworks had been erected on top of the engine and from a large axle ran a series of iron rods of different lengths and at different angles. At the ends of the rods were pewter balls of different sizes painted in bright primary colours. Jangling calliope music came from the box that had been geared up at the side of the steam engine. It hurt Jerry's ears as the rods turned, creaked and jerked to the calliope's rhythm.

Bishop Beesley beamed.

'My own invention, Mr Cornelius; I order the world! I bring realism – the virtues of the past. You see, you are not the only one capable of building a sophisticated machine. This is the model of perfection – the universe, the Utopia that is to come! This is the Beesley Steam Driven Calliopic Orrery! BEHOLD – THE RHYTHM OF THE SPHERES!'

Jerry ran at the machine and was hurled back by Pluto striking him on the side of the jaw. He raised his gun.

But the balls whirled faster and faster and the music shrilled and the steam engine bounced and bellowed. Bishop Beesley waved his pale hands.

'You've thrown it out of control, you nihilist!'

Beesley tried to crawl under the whizzing balls to reach the controls. Jerry lowered his gun.

The balls began to shoot off in all directions. The steam engine screamed. Neptune narrowly missed Jerry's head.

'You have thrown it into chaos!' wailed Beesley.

Jerry was sweating. 'What do you hate? What do you fear?'

The steam engine exploded.

Jerry was hurtled into a field of lilies where a herd of giant antelopes grazed. He got up and kept on running, dodging into Fleet Street's horse-drawn traffic, weaving through the shallows of a tropical river and avoiding mangrove roots and alligators,

loping into Wenceslas Square as Russian tanks burned, and side-stepping into Regents Park Zoo by the Elephant Enclosure. The elephants were dead, their skins blistered by napalm.

But Jerry knew he was home.

The risk had paid off.

He felt a twinge of affection returning already.

6. Brighten Your Night with My Day

Some sectors had been overlooked.

Little monuments of trees, grass and buildings, undamaged by the bombing, stood out against the ash-covered rubble of London.

Jerry recognized a block of flats at Bow, several streets near Hampstead Heath, the public baths and the ABC Cinema at Bayswater, some half-timbered shops where Holborn had run, the British Museum, the Hilton Hotel in Park Lane.

At least a few tourist attractions remained.

Over near the canal eight bulls wheeled in the white sky. Jerry left the zoo and began to tramp across the park, his boots sinking several inches in the fine ash.

Beesley had almost certainly returned to London, but it was anyone's guess where he had set up his headquarters.

Time (in the local sense) was running down at an alarming rate. Beesley was obviously trying to slow the Cycle in order to preserve the present situation and, if possible, return to an earlier phase.

Also it would be disastrous so far as Catherine were concerned. At least his identity was preserved, up to a point. It was his only advantage.

On the other side of a hedge which had been completely stripped of foliage was a neatly parked minihover with British markings.

He resheathed his gun to protect it from the ash and vaulted the hedge.

He opened the minihover's cabin door and climbed in. The thing shifted under his weight. It was armed with two eight inch Banning cannon in Hamilton brackets. The cannon seemed to be low on charges.

The motor started slowly. Jerry rose a few inches in a huge cloud of ash and tilted the joystick forward, heading to where Edgware Road used to be.

He had on a suit of virgin white silk.

Check Temperature

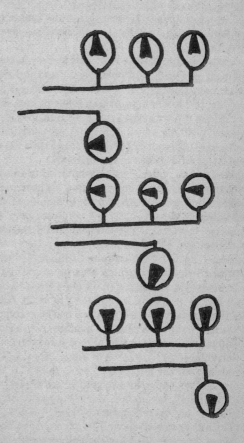

1. What's Wrong with US Medicine

The armoured minihover coughed out of the ash and rode smoothly across the stretch of smooth green crystal. The crystal was what the West End had come to. It wasn't the sort of fusion Jerry liked to see.

As he reached the site of Regent Street, he saw an ashcloud approaching on his left. He guided the minihover into a shallow basin in the crystal and watched. He recognized the jeeps and armoured cars. The Americans were coming back at a lick.

Jerry put the hover's periscope up and adjusted the magnification.

General Ulysses Washington Cumberland stood in the lead jeep, a flame-thrower pack on his back, the nozzle in his right hand. His left hand clutched the windshield, he wore dark combat goggles and his clothes were whipped by the wind. The cap on the general's head bore the legend *C-in-C Europe* and he wore a green, fringed shawl around his shoulders, a long yellow dress with a tight bodice and red buttons, a huge green sash, puffed sleeves, gored skirts and flounces everywhere. The skirt was flared by at least six starched white petticoats and there was a pair of blue tennis shoes on his feet.

Behind General Cumberland the jeeps and cars were filled with fine-featured marines in full battle-kit, here to seek and destroy resistance not cleared out by the bombing.

General Cumberland set an example with his flame thrower. It flared at every possible hiding place.

Jerry shivered. There were signs of snow in the sky. He decided to move on.

As he started the motor he heard Cumberland's voice through his amplifiers.

'They're all queer! Queer! Queer! Queer! Burn 'em out! Out! Out! Out!'

When Jerry reached a higher point on the crystal plain he saw Cumberland leap from his jeep and lead the marines after him.

The flame thrower shrieked again, but Jerry was no longer in range.

Hesitantly some of the marines raised their weapons.

'Sissies! Pansies! Asslickers!' roared the general. He turned, spraying the soldiers with his flame thrower.

'Mother lovers! Mother lovers! You sons of bitches!' he sobbed. In a flurry of frilly underclothes he collapsed on a slab of concrete. There was a WHOOMF, a scream of pure ecstasy, and he went up in a roaring fireball.

At least he died happy, thought Jerry.

The smoke cleared behind him and he saw that the majority of the marines had fried. The rest were trying to put out their burning clothes or their burning vehicles, but then there were a few more explosions and they were finished off.

Jerry admired their energy.

There were flecks of black ash on his suit but it was the sort of price you had to pay.

2. Damned Virgins in the Devil's Lair

The minihover ran out of power sooner than Jerry had expected.

Near the ABC Cinema, Bayswater, he tramped to where an old Riley was parked. As he opened the door a woman with a pale, haggard face looked up at him from the driving seat.

'Can I drop you anywhere, Herr Cornelius?'

'You're still fond of green and purple, I see.'

'It's really all I have left.'

Jerry put his right boot on the nearside wing and began to brush off what remained of the ash. 'Did Beesley send you?'

'I escaped from Beesley.'

'How did you come to leave Amerika?'

'I couldn't stay on top of the job. A general lassitude, I suppose. Maybe I needed you, Jerry. So little new blood. I've become extraordinarily anaemic in recent months. Beesley found me and we flew back to England a few – a few ...'

'Days?'

'Ago.'

'You've changed.'

'You haven't.'

'I should hope not. It's been tough, though. Did Beesley set you up from the beginning?'

'Yes. But I fell in love ...'

'Like a junkie with his dope.' He checked his guilt.

'You weren't the dope I took you for.'

'It's a shame, I know.'

She licked her lips. 'Can I drop you anywhere?' There was a smell about her and it reminded Jerry of Frank.

'I don't think so.'

'Jerry – I need you more than you need me.'

'I know that.'

'I haven't been happy.'

'I can believe that.'

'Just a little, Jerry, understanding ...'

'You have that.'

'Mercy.'

'Sorry, Belle. It's not time to show it.'

She started the engine of the Riley. 'What were you trying to do with the stars?'

'Just hoping to get everything over with quickly. Ragnarok, of sorts.'

'You are fond of Wagner? I, too, am ... Well, maybe not so fond. The end of the world. Is that why you were making all those converts? To make them over with you?'

'Something like that. But you can't impose love ...'

'The world isn't going to end. Beesley's seen to that, hasn't he?'

'He's making a good try.'

'I know why you want the world to end. I hate it, too.'

'It's not as simple as that. I've got a kid sister, you see. I want to give her a better break than I had. A niece, I mean.'

'You're mixed up.'

'Not as much as you, Karen.'

He drew his vibragun. She put her foot on the accelerator. 'Your brake's still on.' The car bounced. Jerry pointed the gun and she shook so much she was soon indistinguishable from the ash. He hooked the green and purple clothes out of the seat with his boot. Poor woman. He didn't know where she'd found the energy in the first place. What had she wanted that she had called 'Love'?

Death? Perhaps, in the end, he had been merciful. He holstered the vibragun and got into her seat. It was very cold.

He didn't feel much warmer himself. The engine was hard to get started again. The motor wouldn't turn. He pumped in more fuel, and it sparked at last.

Through the grey day, through the ruins, he let the car roll straight down the obsidian length of Westbourne Grove.

He had a feeling Beesley was in this area. The bishop had probably sent Karen von Krupp to find him.

He reached the rubble of Ladbroke Grove and the car could move no further. He got out and began to climb over the concrete, between the fronds of twisted wire that had once reinforced it.

He reached the place where the convent had stood and clambered to the highest slab to sniff the scene.

Holland Park was visible. It stood intact on a rise to the south west, its trees ghostly gold and green. Jerry considered it.

A few minutes later, he unsheathed his vibragun from its chamois holster, turned, and, resting the gun on his bent left arm, sighted on a patch of rubble close to the centre of the demolished convent.

The rubble began to quiver and shiver. Then there was nothing left at all but a cloud of dust. Jerry stepped forward and looked into the smooth clearing.

The steel trapdoor was still there. It shone as if burnished. He kneeled on it, pressed his palm against it and murmured a couple of words. The door hissed and took him down twenty feet. He got off and looked up the shaft at the sky. He could see the sun. It had hardly moved.

The steel door ascended and shut off the light.

Jerry depressed a switch. A little illumination flickered for an instant around the room and then died. He moved cautiously through the darkness towards one wall, felt for a shelf above his head and found what he was hoping to find, took out his lighter and by its flame managed to ignite the wick.

He saw that the paraffin was low. He hoped it would last.

The lamp was of blue glass, decorated with gold and scarlet

flowers. It cast shadows around a room full of dusty, alchemical equipment; part of an earlier era. Jerry crossed to a wooden door and pulled it open.

It creaked.

'Mutability.'

He entered a tunnel and the light shone on the semiluminous white coats of half-dead rats. As he pushed his feet through them, they barely moved.

The tunnel was damp and cold and still. By the light of the lamp he saw that his own hands had gone a pale golden colour. He needed sustenance. Beesley must have increased the machine's power. He trod on a rat and it squeaked faintly. 'Mutuality.'

After half a mile the tunnel began to slope upwards until it ended at another steel door. He pressed his hand on it. It didn't move. He murmured the words. The door stayed shut.

With a sigh, Jerry brought out his vibragun. His bones ached.

It took much longer than usual for the gun to disintegrate the steel. Gradually daylight filtered in and there was a hole large enough for Jerry to crawl through. He was in Holland Park, close to the Belvedere Restaurant which had once been part of Holland House and had included the orangery.

He had left in the afternoon. Now it was morning. Did Beesley realize how senseless his plan was? An abuse of the power.

He thought of Catherine and began to run.

'Love!'

3. So You Want to be a Rock and Roll Star?

As he reached the Elizabethan façade of Holland House, Jerry paused and looked up.

The American jets were dancing in the frozen sky. For several minutes they performed complicated formations then regrouped into conventional flights and flew away from London towards the Atlantic. Either they had been recalled or events had got on top of them.

With mixed feelings Jerry watched them leave.

He was on his own now.

Pushing open the mansion's heavy doors he entered a large, gloomy hall. A Shifter gateway had once been here, but he knew it must have dispersed by now. Beesley had buggered the phasing completely.

He drew his gun and started up the Tudor staircase.

Mitzi was waiting, unarmed, at the top. She wore an ankle-length dress in Regency stripes of dark and light pink. There were pink slippers on her feet and her blonde hair was combed to frame her face. Her large blue eyes regarded him.

'Herr Cornelius. You are not looking well.'

'I'm as well as could be expected.' He motioned with the vibragun. 'Is Beesley here?'

'My father? Yes. He's waiting for you. He thinks you're probably ready to join us at last.'

She smiled and Jerry saw that her teeth seemed to have grown to points, like a fox's. 'It will soon be summer again, and we can be together . . .' She turned, walking back along the landing. 'This way.'

Jerry hesitated.

'What's the matter?' She paused by the door of the main bedroom.

'Death.' His nostrils quivered. 'A lot of death.'

'There's nothing wrong with death. Nothing to be afraid of. A sleep . . .'

'It depends on the kind.' He gripped the gun desperately.

'Don't you like the idea of life after death?'

'It depends on the kind.'

'Herr Cornelius, you have no *trust*.' Her eyes widened with sympathy. 'You are so wild.'

'I ...' He felt very tired.

'You are a fierce beast.'

'No ...'

'You must be more tame. In time.'

'I want ...' He gasped as the tears flooded from his face. 'I want ...'

'Peace. We want nothing more.'

'Peace?'

He rocked on his heels. His grip was still tight on his gun, though all his energy seemed concentrated in his right hand.

She came towards him. He tried to raise his gun. She stretched out her palm. He shook his head.

'Don't you want to rest? We can help you rest.'

'Not that kind. Not – retreat ...'

She frowned, her eyes concerned. 'Why do you split hairs so? Does it matter about the kind?'

'Yes.'

'We all grow older, you know. More mature.'

'No.'

'Love,' said Mitzi. 'Do you have nothing but your Cause? It is hopeless, you know.'

'Love.' The tears chilled his cheeks. He trembled as he thought of Oxford and Catherine and the Science of Innocence.

'You know,' Mitzi murmured, 'that what you have done is wrong. But we forgive you.'

He snarled and laughed through his teeth. The energy left his right hand and blazed from his eyes. 'I am Jerry Cornelius.' The gun dropped. He bent but she swept forward and kicked the gun through the banisters and he watched it fall slowly to the floor of the hall below.

'It's a turning world, darling.' Mitzi helped him straigthen up, wincing as she saw his eyes. 'There are many kinds of beauty.'

Jerry staggered back from her with a growl.

The cardinal came out of the master bedroom. 'Misericordia! The poor chap looks completely beaten. He needs help.'

Jerry tried to descend the stairs. It was dawn outside. He gasped as the cardinal seized him around the waist.

'Could you bring him in here, please, Cardinal Orelli.' Mitzi's voice was vibrant with sympathy. 'He'll soon feel a new man.'

Jerry shut everything down.

He let them get on with it. He had given himself up.

'Le Commandant'
7-IN-1 JEWELED SWISS CHRONOGRAPH
Amazing wrist watch 'command post!'

Actually 7 watches in 1 – complete with 6 dials, 5 hands, 2 pushbutton controls! A miracle of Swiss watchmaking ingenuity. Genuine Swiss-calibrated, anti-magnetic movement keeps perfect time plus many more functions! Use it as a stop watch. Measure distance. Check parking meters. Register speed – car or boat. Check production figures. Take time, motion studies or time the number of beers consumed in an hour! Set dial as 'wrist watch secretary.' Unlimited uses! Get yours today direct from the Swiss Fabrique at giant savings.

Pay only $12.95, an unconditional money-back GUARANTEE.

Hilton Watch Company ad, *Confidential Detective*

1. One Too Many Mornings

He was awakened by a cold caress.

Mitzi's waxen hand was on his brow. He felt the heat leave his head and he tried to jerk away.

She removed her hand.

He lay on a hard mattress in a wide four-poster with grey curtains that were drawn back so that he could see Bishop Beesley standing by the Jacobean dresser and bending over the box which stored Jerry's machine.

Ash-coloured light came through the window. Jerry took stock of his reserves. They were low.

'Good – um – hello, there, Mr Cornelius. I see my daughter's been looking after you. She's an angel. A ministering angel.'

Jerry sat up. He was still dressed in his white suit and he was unbound. He frowned suspiciously at Mitzi.

'I'm sick,' he said, 'of ...'

'Cancer?' said Mitzi.

'Crabs.'

'It's a complicated state of affairs, I'm afraid,' said the bishop, chewing a Crunchie bar. The artificial honeycomb coursed down his chins. 'I've got so far, but I now need your help. I want to find out where the rest of your "converts" are, for a start. Some are hanging on, you know, against all common sense.'

'I promised them nothing less than the Millennium.' Jerry drew a sluggish breath. 'What do you expect?'

'I'm afraid we'll have to put back the Millennium for a while.' Beesley smacked his lips. 'I know it's disappointing. They were all prepared for it, weren't they? Well, that's over. If you can help me locate them, I'll get in touch with them and arrange a deconversion. Could I say fairer?'

Jerry took a lock of his hair in his hand. It was stringy and off-white. He sniffed. 'Cut cocaine.'

'You knew the apocalypse wasn't due for several million years yet, Mr Cornelius,' Bishop Beesley continued, 'and yet you wished to bring it about for purely selfish reasons. Reasons, I regret, that I simply fail to understand. It may be all right for you – but consider your dupes!'

'What do you think my crash programme was for?' Jerry glanced out of the window. A wind was blowing the ash northward.

'You can't save the whole human race, Mr Cornelius. Besides, I insist that your motives were still suspect, let alone your goals!'

Jerry got off the bed and walked weakly to the box but Mitzi barred his way, looking questioningly at her father. Bishop Beesley shrugged. 'We've reached something of an impasse, I'm afraid. The power seems to be weakening.'

'You can say that again.' Jerry smiled. 'What else did you expect?'

Bishop Beesley cast down his eyes in embarrassment and unwrapped a toffee. 'I never claimed to be a scientist, Mr Cornelius.'

'Naturally.' Jerry stroked the box. 'You'll have to find a power source, won't you? Whether transmission of any kind's possible now, I just don't know. Things are fixed, Bishop Beesley. They are solid.'

'The sun hasn't moved for an – for some t—' Mitzi gave up. 'It isn't moving.'

'That's merely an indication,' Jerry said. 'An image, if you like. I'm going to have to think ...'

'What sort of power does the machine take?' Beesley asked, chewing. 'Electricity?'

Jerry laughed as best he could. 'I'm afraid not. It runs on primitive energy. It's all very basic, when you get down to it.'

'Where do we get this energy?'

'Is Cardinal Orelli still on the premises?'

'I think he went to the lavatory.'

'Never mind. Ask him in when he's finished, will you?'

'Herr Cornelius,' Mitzi whispered, 'you must explain to us everything. You must not make mysteries. It is a time for frankness. You will admit that you have no choice now.'

'Frankness.' Jerry drew a deep breath. 'You said it. Bring Cardinal Orelli in as soon as you can. I'm very tired. Time's slipping by. I need a long rest.'

'I think I heard him on the landing.' Bishop Beesley opened

the door. 'Ah, cardinal. Would you step in here a moment please?'

Cardinal Orelli smiled at Jerry. 'How are you, my son?'

'How do you feel, cardinal?' Jerry asked.

'Very well.'

'Good.' Jerry opened the lid of the box and moved a plate set in the bottom left corner. It was about four inches wide and six inches long and eight inches deep, lined with a rubbery substance. 'Would you place your hands together, cardinal? Palm against palm.'

The cardinal smiled and assumed a praying position.

'That's fine. Now put the hands into the slot there. Don't worry, it won't hurt you.'

The cardinal glanced at the bishop who nodded. Mitzi's lips parted, her eyes shone. The cardinal dipped his hands into the slot up to the wrists, the box hummed briefly, the cardinal's lifeless body crumpled to the floor.

'It's fuelled again,' said Beesley, bending over the gauge. 'Good heavens!'

'It won't last long,' said Jerry. He turned a knob and gripped a metal bar positioned in the centre.

A shock raced through him and he felt a little sick, but he kicked Beesley in the crutch so that he fell back into Mitzi's arms, picked up the box and made for the door.

They yelled at him as he raced down the stairs, paused in the hall to recover his vibragun and dashed out into the grey day.

He was using up energy very quickly, in spite of everything. He stumbled down the steps, through the gates, out over the cricket pitch, his boots sinking in ash, and behind him came Bishop Beesley and Mitzi who had paused only to get their Remingtons.

In the middle of the cricket pitch he fell and the box flew from his arms. He choked on the ash.

He tried to get up but collapsed, rolled over on his back to get his vibragun out, but already Mitzi and Bishop Beesley were standing over him, their rifles pointing at his heart.

'We'll have to manage on our own now that we know how to keep the machine's strength up.'

Apologetically, Bishop Beesley squeezed the trigger.

There was a pop and a slithering noise and a bullet fell out of the barrel. Mitzi pulled her trigger and the same thing happened. Her bullet fell in Jerry's lap. He felt a mild shock in his right ball.

Mitzi raised her head at the sound of barking. Bishop Beesley followed her gaze.

Coming across the ash, her head and body swathed in white furs, driving a sled pulled by a team of a dozen dogs, including two St Bernards, a borzoi and three salukis, was a tall woman armed with a steel bow and a quiver of alloy arrows. Close by she stopped the dogs and they flung themselves down panting. She fitted an arrow to her bow.

'I wonder if you'd let Mr Cornelius rise?' said the woman in the white fur.

They stepped back and Jerry got up, dusting ash off his suit.

The new arrival motioned with her brow. 'What I'd like to know, bishop – I take it you are a bishop – is what you think you're accomplishing, fucking about with the sun and so forth.

'I'm trying to put things right,' Beesley said sullenly. 'I'm a journalist by trade.' He studied the woman's weapons, obviously attempting to decide if the bow and arrow were as ineffective as his rifle.

'A bow has more power, at short range, than an ordinary rifle,' said the tall figure.

'How much more power?' asked Mitzi.

'Quite a bit.'

Mitzi sucked at her lower lip.

Jerry went down on his knees beside the box and began to drag it through the grey dust towards the sled. It took him a while to load it aboard. 'I hope I'm not overburdening you,' he said to the newcomer.

'I'd allowed for the extra. They're good dogs.'

'I suppose you haven't ...'

'Do you want it now?'

'I think I'd better.'

'Look under the skin nearest you.'

Jerry pulled back the wolfskin and there was a little replica of one of his webs. He switched it on and it began to pipe. He buried his head in it. 'That's more like it.'

'It was the best I could do,' said the woman in the white furs. 'But it's the last. You'll be on your own soon.'

Jerry straightened up.

The sun had started to move again.

2. I'm so Glad

The sled slid away across the cricket pitch.

Behind it Mitzi and Bishop Beesley sat slumped in the ash. Mitzi had pulled up her skirt and seemed to be inspecting her inner thigh. Her father was unwrapping a Milky Way.

'You seem very fit,' Jerry said to his companion as she whipped up the dogs.

'Fitter than ever.' They gathered speed. 'I took the opportunity of diverting some of the energy to myself while that chap was trying to do whatever it was he was trying to do.'

'So that's what happened to it. I couldn't understand ...'

'It turned out for the best, I think you'll agree.'

'You can say that again.'

'Where to now?'

'Oxford, I think.'

'Okay. I suppose it was wise, was it, to leave that pair where they are?'

'Oh, I don't think they'll be much trouble now. Poor things – if we succeed, they'll hardly survive the transformation.'

'Quite.'

The runners scraped the ash and they rode in silence for a few miles until they reached the outskirts of London and the ash gave way to the asphalt of the M40. The dogs were cut from their traces and lay down panting.

Una Persson pushed back her hood and pointed to an intersection and a hotel called The Jolly Englishman which stood beside a garage. 'That's where I left the car.'

Pulling the sled behind them, they made for The Jolly Englishman, followed by the pack of dogs.

Jerry checked his watches. They were ticking perfectly. He was relieved, though there were still a great many uncertainties. It was difficult to work out in his head what side-effects Beesley's attempts had initiated.

A counter-revolution, after all, was a counter-revolution.

They carried the equipment to the big Duesenburg and

stowed it down by the back seats. Una Persson got into the car and started the engine. Jerry sat beside her and slammed the door.

The dogs began to howl.

'Faithful buggers,' said Una. 'But there's nothing else for it, I'm afraid.' She turned the car on to the M40 and drove towards Oxford.

'It does you good to get out of London occasionally,' said Jerry as the evening sunlight touched the red leaves of the elms lining the road.

'Especially at this time of the year,' agreed Mrs Persson.

'Have all the Americans gone home now?'

'I think so. Your mum's a bit fed up about it. Beesley's messing about didn't help matters, of course. A general panic over there, by the sound of it. Just as things were settling down nicely, too.' Una turned on the tape machine and got John, George, Paul and Ringo doing *She's Leaving Home*.

Jerry relaxed.

3. I Don't Live Today

Una Persson pulled off her furs and stretched herself out on the yellow silks of the bed in the Oxford underground pied-à-terre.

'This is a bit more like it. Hasn't changed much, has it?'

'Some things don't. Not very often, at any rate.' Jerry poured two glasses of Pernod. 'You're still fond of this, I hope.'

She extended an arm that glowed with energy. 'You can bet your life. Thanks.' She sipped the Pernod. 'I'm not particularly thirsty, but it's nice just to taste. I think I could go off martyrdom.'

'I know what you mean.'

'Could I have a last look at Catherine, Jerry? Would you mind?'

Jerry felt a pang of jealousy. 'Of course not.'

They walked down the corridor together, entered the morgue, opened Catherine's drawer and looked down at her lovely face. 'As beautiful as ever,' murmured Una. 'It's been a long time.'

Jerry patted her shoulder.

'I wish ...' Mrs Persson turned away. 'Still, I shouldn't be here at all. Maybe it wasn't wise ...' She walked swiftly from the morgue, leaving Jerry to put the drawer back and close the door.

When Jerry returned to the room, Una Persson had taken off all her clothes and was sitting on the edge of the bed staring at the console and tapping her knees.

'Can we get it over with now?' she said.

Jerry lifted the box and put it between them. He slid back the slot covering and with his red silk handkerchief he wiped it carefully. Then he stared straight into her eyes. 'Cheerio. Thanks for everything. I've been Harlequin for long enough.

'Cheerio, Jerry.'

She put her hands together and shoved them quickly into the slot. Her lips parted over clenched teeth, her body began to sag, her complexion to dull, her hair to lose its lustre. She breathed more and more slowly until she stopped, but her hands still remained in the slot until her flesh shrank and her skin turned yellow and there was little more than a skeleton lying beside the machine.

Jerry picked the corpse up and carried it in one hand to the morgue, filing it in the spare drawer furthest from Catherine's. Then he went back and inspected the machine.

Una had been carrying a huge supply of energy and the machine was charged to capacity, but the energy in itself wouldn't be enough to bring Catherine back for more than a few minutes. Much more energy had to be released and then channelled to give Catherine the life Jerry wanted her to have.

It would require a massive build up and release of energy and this meant speeding up the time cycle (or what was left of

it). Only those with their identities firmly established would survive the spin.

He felt lonely as he prepared the machine. But then he forgot his loneliness in his anticipation.

He brought Catherine in and laid her on the bed. He bolted the box to the bench he had assembled. He ran a thin pipe from the box to Catherine's throat and secured it with a piece of surgical tape.

He checked his instruments carefully.

Then he turned on.

Respiration Check

'Mind you, this is in Brisbane, well south in Queensland. Melbourne, 1200 miles further down, gets very variable weather and can get nippy days even in the middle of summer. Shocking place. Unreliable. But 1200 miles to the north, up past the Tropic of Capricorn, lies Cairns – beaches, palm trees, Great Barrier Reef, free coconuts, tropical paradise, the coming tourist Mecca of the Pacific. And still in Queensland, which is over $2\frac{1}{2}$ times as big as Texas. How about that? And contains perhaps two million people – how about *that*? Away from the cities a man can often drive for miles without sighting another human being. Smog? What smog? Colour problem? What colour problem? Population explosion? Jesus, you have to be kidding!'

Jack Wodhams, letter to *SFWA Bulletin*

1. The Stranger on the Whole Road

Jerry increased the power and checked that all dimensions could be phased in at the right moment. He synched Jimi Hendrix in. He began to sing *Third Stone from the Sun* very loudly. It was all part of the ritual; all part of the spell.

And it was a tense moment.

He twisted his head to look at Catherine, and set the pointer to Automatic.

Things began to hum.

Swiftly Jerry increased the entropy rate to maximum, preparing himself for the ensuing dissipation.

He began to feel dizzy as he gave the universe a whirl. For all the shielding in his lab, he wondered if he were safe after all. He blinked and could see the leaping cord that led to Catherine's throat, saw Catherine's body tremble.

He adjusted the identity stabilizers and locked in the coordinates. There was now a golden mist swirling everywhere and the box had become very hot.

When everything was on Full he fell backwards and on to and then through the bed and continued to fall.

He pulled himself together as best he could. It didn't matter about the extent of the dispersal so long as he kept everything in the right order. He began to flood through the universe and then through the multiverse, to the sounds of the Beatles singing *A Day in the Life*, throbbing in time to the cosmic pulse. Universe upon universe; dimension upon dimension; they spread out together and the extraneous energy released in the explosion poured into the box and into Catherine's body.

Faster and faster flew the particles and Jerry hung on. Framed against the spreading gases he saw other human shapes and he knew that some of the transmogs were managing to resist the conversion of the universe.

He looked about him and waited as *Helter Skelter* echoed through the infinite. It was quite a nice trip.

At last maximum diffusion was reached and everything became a little unreal. He felt a moment's concern before the switch clicked over, Jimi Hendrix started to play *Are You Experienced?*, and things began to come together again.

Soon he would know if the experiment had paid off.

Or was it all an illusion? Or a model?

2. A Sweet Little Schooner

Jerry took a deep breath, opened his eyes and saw springs moving. He was under the bed. He rolled out and there was his machine steaming on the bench. Its circuits appeared to have fused. He activated the tv monitors and got the surface.

The towers of the Cathedral were white against the white sky. It was snowing. It was only to be expected. Otherwise Oxford looked pretty much as it had always looked.

With a sigh, he looked down at the bed. Catherine turned uncomfortably in her sleep, her long-fingered hands at her throat.

Jerry ripped off the surgical tape and threw the cord aside. 'Catherine?'

She sniffed and moistened her lips. Then she woke up. 'Jerry? Are you all right?'

'I think so. I had a bit of a turn a moment ago, but I'm fine now. How about you?'

'I thought I was dead.'

'What's death? An absence! I've been experimenting for months.'

'It was nice of you, Jerry.'

'Frank, by the way, won't be bothering us.'

'Oh, good. I was wondering about that.' She got up. They were very much alike. 'You've turned quite pale, Jerry.'

'It's for the best, I suppose.'

Operation Successful

Infant Stars

Each year two or three new stars are born within the Milky Way. They appear to condense out of dark globules of dust. Knowledge of how this happens would reveal much about the way galaxies – and the universe itself – were formed.

Science Journal, July 1968

1. The Olfactory Code

Apart from a tendency from time to time to imagine he heard various forms of audiosignals together with the voices of Karen von Krupp, of Bishop and Mitzi Beesley and of Frank, Jerry felt no ill effects. There was a touch of his old paramnesia, too, but, if anything, that was reassuring.

He and Catherine wandered hand in hand through Holland Park. Harlequin and Colombine.

It was their last day together.

Jerry was wearing his green silk suit, yellow silk shirt and red boots. Catherine's outfit, with its full length skirt, matched his.

Holland Park was covered in snow. Long, glassy white icicles hung on the columns of the fountain and there was thick ice on the pond. The tropical evergreens sheltered the peacocks and guinea fowl while pigeons, sparrows, robins and blackbirds flew about looking for food. It was a peaceful day.

Over on the cricket pitch Catherine noticed two new statues. 'I haven't seen those before.'

As she led Jerry across the pitch they left black footprints in their wake.

They reached the statues.

Mitzi and Bishop Beesley had been transformed into the purest grey marble.

'Who are they, Jerry? There isn't a plaque.'

'I'll get one fixed up. They're two people who achieved their hearts' desires. There's no looking back for them now. They look pretty permanent don't they?'

'They do indeed. So natural.'

Jerry ran his hand over Bishop Beesley's marble paunch and stroked his marble Mars Bar. Affectionately he patted Mitzi's cool brow. 'It's what they would have wanted.'

In the middle-distance they saw the sharp outlines of Holland House. The light was very clear; the sky pure blue and the trees cast clean, black shadows on the white ground. They began to return, strolling past wooden benches piled high with snow, through the orangery, down the covered walk and stopping to look at the clock-tower that stood among the chimneys and the spires of the house.

'I feel very warm,' said Catherine.

'You *are* very warm,' said Jerry.

She lay down in the snowdrops and Jerry slowly took off her clothes and then his own. They made love for a long time until the snow had melted for several yards in all directions and the grass beneath was fresh and bright.

The sun got low and Catherine died again.

Jerry stood up shivering. He looked down at her with affection but without sorrow. He climbed into his own clothes and folded hers up and put them beside her. Love could conquer all.

Then he walked away from there, leaving her lying surrounded by the snow. It had all been worthwhile. He felt a new person.

There was still work to be done. He had to find a new way to get back on the job.

And then there was the baby to consider. He could feel it stirring already. He would have to relax, to rest.

Jerry left the park. He stood by the gates and looked across the vast plain of ice to where he could see his sled. He trudged towards it, breathing in the crisp air.

At his approach the eager dogs scrambled up panting. He assembled them in their positions, patted the head of the leader, a Great Dane, and shoved the sled so that its runners broke from the ice and it slid easily, gathering speed.

He jumped in, cracked his whip, grinned at the sun as the wind rushed past. The dogs leaned in their traces.

There had to be a method of maintaining equilibrium without this constant shifting of weights. Guilt was what did it, he supposed.

He said: 'Mush.'